Bob Gray's
ATTACK OF THE
MELONHEADS

Novelization by
Solon Tsangaras and Gary Lee Vincent

Burning Bulb
PUBLISHING

Attack of the Melonheads
Screenplay by **Bob Gray**
Novelization by **Solon Tsangaras** and **Gary Lee Vincent**
Edited by **Wol-vriey**

Burning Bulb Publishing
P.O. Box 4721
Bridgeport, WV 26330-4721
United States of America
www.BurningBulbPublishing.com

Cover illustration by Sarah Lynn.

First Edition.

Paperback Edition ISBN: 978-0692535844

Printed in the United States of America

Dedicated to
Lady Gray

Hydrocephalus:
1. A condition in which fluid accumulates in the brain, typically in young children, enlarging the head and sometimes causing brain damage.

CHAPTER ONE
Kirtland, Ohio, 1964

Lightning flashed and rain seemed to fall in buckets as the ambulance sped down the road. Its lone occupant, Dr. Malcolm Crowe, pressed the accelerator harder, almost challenging the weather to stop his newly-purchased 1964 International Harvester ambulance. He would like to have purchased the new Cadillac ambulance, but the I.H. was a more logical and efficient choice. He raced past the cemetery, half of a smile showing from the dashboard lights. "Not tonight", he said to the headstones, as the vehicle sped along the road, making the fence nothing but a blur. Just past the cemetery, Dr. Crowe saw the familiar sign, Cuyahoga Clinic, and pulled into the gate, slowing down slightly as he maneuvered along the manicured lawn and shrubbery lining the quarter-mile ride to the clinic. He noticed a single light shining from the building as he pulled up to the main entrance.

Dr. Crowe opened the door of the ambulance, which was whipped from his hands by a giant gust of wind. He got out of the vehicle and slammed the heavy door with one hand and, with the other, struggled to keep his fedora on his head. He clutched his long coat, trying his best to keep it closed as he approached the massive entrance doors to the building. Without knocking, he opened one of the doors and stepped inside, shaking off the damp rain. He focused his attention on the long marble hallway, and the light glowing from behind one of the doors at the end. He straightened himself, and, seemingly oblivious to the muffled moans coming from the room, hurried down the hall to Room 213.

"I'm in here, Doc," came a voice from behind the closed door. Not surprised, Dr. Crowe reached for the doorknob and entered the room.

"What the hell took you so long?" asked Eddie, the eighteen-year-old intern, as he leaned harder against the closet door. There was a pounding from the other side of the door, mixed with screams and strange gurgling sounds, as if whatever was on the other side wanted to get out.

Eddie could never get used to looking at them. They didn't live long, 10 years at the most, but, on a few occasions, some came in as teenagers. With their swollen, water-filled heads, and eyes that bulged from the sides of their heads (almost like parakeets, Eddie once joked), he did not want to be in the same room with them for very long. At all, if he had his choice.

"I came as soon as I could," replied Dr. Crowe, the eagerness in his eyes showing. "How many this time?" He walked toward the closet door, not flinching as the pounding increased.

Eddie wasted no time in responding. "Three. Two boys and one girl." He nodded toward the door. "I was able to sedate the first two pretty easily, but the needle broke on the big one." He turned to the doctor, a wry smile breaking through. "He's a little-upset."

Stepping closer, Dr. Crowe leaned against the frame of the closet door as the moaning from the other side ebbed, then continued louder than before. "Whom do I owe?" he asked, eying the closet.

"County brought 'em in."

"Any family?" Crowe asked, almost as a formality, not that it would have made a difference.

"Nope. Orphans. Nobody's gonna claim THESE freaks." There was a hint of glee in Eddie's voice as he leaned harder on the closet door. "Nobody knows they even exist."

Dr. Crowe removed his wallet from the inside of his jacket and removed three one-hundred-dollar bills from the side pouch, neatly placing them on the table. He looked at Eddie with each bill placement.

Eddie shook his head and smiled. "The price went up, Doc. It's one hundred and FIFTY each now."

Dr. Crowe's eyes widened. "What?" he asked, incredulously.

Eddie shrugged. "It's not like you're buying gas here, Doc. These are PEOPLE. Children." As an afterthought, he added, "And it's a seller's market."

He stared at Eddie, not quite angry, because this was out of Eddie's 'jurisdiction'. "Thank those bloodsuckers for me," he said, as he peeled off another hundred-dollar bill and a single fifty.

He looked up at Eddie, and pulled another fifty, and added it to the pile of money. "And thank YOU, Eddie," he said, as he put away his billfold.

Eddie smiled, but didn't stop applying pressure against the closet door. He gestured to a pole with a noose leaning in a corner. "Grab that noose over there."

As Dr. Crowe retrieved the pole, Eddie pointed to the loop. "Make it bigger", he said. As the doctor adjusted the loop, Eddie shook his head. "Bigger than that, Doc."

Crowe's eyes widened. "Really?" He opened the loop twice more, looking at Eddie each time, until Eddie nodded in satisfaction. Eddie adjusted his position in front of the closet door, almost like a football linebacker getting ready for a play.

"Okay, get ready," he warned. "Here he comes." He grabbed the doorknob and slowly turned it. The sound of the lock disengaging momentarily silenced the ruckus behind the door.

With a nod, Eddie whipped open the closet door. The sudden burst of light inside the dark closet blinded the 'occupant', a 13-year-old child, but with a grossly misshapen head, swollen to close to three times the size of a normal child. Lying on the floor behind him were two more unconscious children, one boy, one girl, obviously younger, but both with equally deformed craniums.

The 'child' charged blindly from the closet straight toward Dr. Crowe, who expertly threw the noose around its neck. The giant hydrocephalic head of the child snapped left and right as he struggled to free himself from the noose. As the doctor used all of his strength to control the child, Eddie sneaked up behind him and jabbed him in the neck with a hypodermic filled to capacity with a strong sedative. The child continued to struggle for fifteen seconds, with Dr.

Crowe's expression showing concern that the sedative was not working, but slowly, ever so slowly, the deformed head began to loll from side to side, finally succumbing to the anesthesia.

Not wasting time with three separate trips using gurneys, Eddie brought in a wheelbarrow and loaded the three 'acquisitions' onto it, and followed Dr. Crowe down the dark corridor to the front door, where the ambulance had been backed up as close as it could get. They loaded the children into the back, and the doctor tossed several sheets over the prone bodies, not to keep them warm, but in case prying eyes should happen to glance into the vehicle.

"How long 'til the sedative wears off?" he asked, as he slammed the back door of the ambulance closed.

"Couple hours," Eddie replied.

Crowe walked around to the drivers' side door. As Crowe opened the door of the ambulance, Eddie looked up. He had been recounting his money. "We can't keep doing this, Doc. Sooner or later someone's gonna find out what—"

The doctor interrupted. "I can handle Dr. Reilly, Eddie." "He's not a problem." He sat down behind the wheel and looked up at Eddie. "Besides, this should be all I need."

Eddie finished counting the money and as he slipped it into his pocket. He gestured toward the back of the ambulance: "Dr. Crowe What *are* you doing with them?"

With an obviously fake smile, Dr. Crowe looked up at Eddie. "I'm treating them," he reassured. With that, he closed the door of the ambulance, put it in gear, and sped off into the rainy night.

As the taillights of the vehicle disappeared from view, Eddie looked down the dark driveway. "I pray to God that he never has to treat ME!"

The ride back to the Crowe mansion took longer than usual due to the inclement weather but the International Harvester cruised through with no problem. Branches and other debris littered the road as Dr. Crowe piloted his new ambulance along the road, finally reaching his residence.

'Mansion' was an appropriate word to describe the Crowe estate. It was huge, reminiscent of an old European castle, and was set nearly half a mile up a long, winding seasonal driveway, surrounded by a thick, lush maple forest.

Crowe turned into the gates and raced to the rear entrance of the building, where the loading door to his laboratory was located. He parked the ambulance as close as he could to the house.

Taking a cue from Eddie, he brought over his own wheelbarrow and loaded the unconscious forms of the hydrocephalic children onto it. Carefully, he brought them inside. When he got them into the mansion, he wheeled them to a large main floor-to-basement dumb-waiter, usually used to transport heavy groceries from one floor to another, which was big enough to hold the two smaller bodies easily.

Two trips later, the children were downstairs in Dr. Crowe's private 'facility.' Each was strapped to his or her own individual tables. The doctor worked his way around the room, where other 'patients' were secured to similar tables. Some were connected to intravenous lines and some had tubes coming from their bodies.

After a quick check of the room, he walked to the stairs, turned off the light and closed the door.

From the living room Dr. Crowe's wife, Marilyn, paced nervously as the moans of those that were downstairs echoed up from the basement laboratory. Marilyn was a beautiful woman, not looking a bit her 34 years, with a kind, gentle heart. It was obvious by the look on her face as her husband entered the room, that she was distraught.

Her husband knew what she was going to say, having brought it up countless times before, but each time he brought home new 'house guests', the conversation would again begin anew. He was correct.

"Please, Malcolm", she said. "Anywhere but here."

Crowe had been through this conversation before and had the answers ready. "I can't give them the help they need at the clinic," he said. "There are too many restrictions there."

Marilyn did not back down. "Malcolm, it's our CELLAR, NOT a hospital ward!" The cacophony from downstairs was a brutal soundtrack to her words. "Is THIS what I'm going to have to listen to every day?" She gestured toward the entrance to the basement, a single tear of frustration running down her soft cheek.

Crowe walked up to her, gently placing a hand on one shoulder, while the other brushed away that tear. Smiling, he said, "They'll calm down in a bit, once they get used to their surroundings."

Marilyn pulled away. "What am I supposed to do, Malcolm?"

Crowe straightened up and softly gazed into his wife's eyes. "Just let me do my work," he said, almost in a condescending whisper. "Believe me, if there was a better way to do this, I would." There was an almost bitter defiance in his stance, which did not go with his words.

Marilyn noticed this and briefly paused, staring into her husband's eyes. Her expression began to soften.

Suddenly, the moment was interrupted by a series of wails and moans from the cellar. That soft expression quickly reverted back to defiant hardness.

"You're going to owe me," she grumbled.

Crowe smiled. "Thank you, darling." He walked over to her and took her hand. "Whatever you want."

Marilyn let out a small yawn. "Right now, I would like some sleep." As she turned and walked toward the grand staircase leading to the master bedroom, Malcolm Crowe decided to try something.

"Would you like meet them?" he said, as she reached the stairs.

Marilyn was almost startled by the question. "Meet them?"

Their eyes met as he smiled and nodded. *She's softening up to them*, Crowe thought. *Perfect*.

Lightening flashed from the raging storm outside.

Almost as if in sync with the storm, Crowe reached out his hand to Marilyn. She took it and they both walked to the stairs leading to the basement laboratory.

CHAPTER TWO
Fifty years later

Nearly fifty years of growth have made the lush maple forest around the old Crowe mansion look like an Amazon rain forest, encroaching on the actual building. The mansion had lost its grandeur, though, its stone foundation the only thing remaining, standing defiantly against the elements. Most of the residents of Downtown Kirtland considered it haunted, which is why they give it a very wide berth.

Most, with one exception of Claudio Oliveri. Claudio was an Italian immigrant who left his native Italy some 20 years ago to start a wine business in the United States, but somehow landed in Ohio tapping maple trees. His tall, lanky body snaked through the maple forest surrounding the former Crowe mansion, checking his lucrative and expansive maple 'employees', making sure they were tapped properly and producing that delicious liquid 'fortune.' He collected the full aluminum buckets, and made his way back to his little pick-up truck, buckets clanking with each step, but he never spilled a drop.

His rounds usually took up the better part of his morning and when he was done, he would go into town and wave to everyone as he drove along the road.

Downtown Kirtland was a small town, very charming and reminiscent of a bygone era. People felt safe as they walked down the street, whether they were purchasing items from the locally-owned stores or just window-shopping. Its wholesome appearance was amplified by all the businesses that were on the main drag. Unlike the more modern, bustling bigger towns, Main Street in Downtown Kirtland was home to a doctor's office, *The Kirtland Stinger*, which was the local paper that EVERYONE quoted their 'facts' from, and even the local police station sat comfortably amongst the shops.

Chief Dooley spent the last 23 years of his life in the Kirtland Police Department, joining in 1992 at the ripe age of 37. After working various jobs across the country, he wound up back home in Kirtland, taking a job at *The Stinger* before deciding he would be best suited as a law enforcement officer. He quickly became police chief, and, in all his years on the job, never drew his firearm.

Downtown Kirtland was bustling this afternoon, with some of the older folks strolling around town, gossiping (which meant 'quoting from *The Stinger*').

Dooley heard the familiar rumble of Claudio's pick-up truck and glanced down the street as he approached. He maneuvered his formidable frame down the three steps of the police station and walked to the curb just as Claudio drove by. Claudio waved frantically at the Chief, smiling, and motioned for him to come to his vehicle as he pulled up to the curb.

Dooley walked up to Claudio, grinning as he peeked into the back of his pick-up. "Collecting more sap for your syrup empire?" asked Dooley, as Claudio spryly popped out from the driver's seat.

"Si, Chief Dooley. I love it," he replied taking in a deep breath and patting his chest. "Fresh air, nature all around." Dooley smiled at the heavy Italian accent, which had not dissipated at all in all the years he's known Claudio. "Bella!"

Glancing at his watch, Dooley walked around Claudio to the squad car, but that didn't stop the effervescent Claudio from his 'dissertation.'

"You know, Chief Dooley, when I live in Italy, my family, all day long, make a GREAT vino", he began.

Dooley had heard this all before, but there was nothing he could do to stop it. He smiled at Claudio. "Yeah, yeah. You told me that."

Claudio went on. "But the grape here in Ohio not as good as Italia grape." With each word, Dooley mouthed what Claudio was saying, having heard this speech over a dozen times.

"Yeah, we already discussed this."

"Si", said Claudio, "but YOU, Chief Dooley. You tell me forget about vino and teach me about this 'maple syrup'." He smiled proudly. "So now I have two THOUSAND bottles ready for the stores." As he spoke, he reached into his pocket with his sap-soaked gloved hand, producing a small—no, TINY—bottle of syrup. "And I want YOU to have the very first bottle." Dooley smiled as Claudio proudly presented his gift.

"That's a pretty small bottle", Dooley said with a smirk.

"Five dollars." Claudio stood almost at attention. "It's very good!"

Dooley reached for the bottle. "Must be, for five

bucks." As Dooley took the bottle from Claudio, his glove came right off, attached to the bottle that was sticky with fresh sap.

As Claudio peeled his glove from the bottle that Dooley was holding, he meekly said, "Oh, sorry. I forgot my sticky gloves."

When the glove was safely extracted from the minuscule bottle, Dooley raised it as if to toast. "Thank you, Claudio."

As Claudio walked away from Chief Dooley, putting his sticky glove back on, Doctor Reilly, the resident physician, appeared in the doorway of his office. He ran his hand along his upper lip, trying to tame his bristly mustache. He had spent his entire life in Kirtland, being the only doctor there for the last 50 years. His casual, yet dignified demeanor made him one of the most-liked residents of the area.

Just as Claudio was stepping back into his pick-up truck, Dooley opened the door to the police cruiser and called to Claudio. "Claudio! Where are you tapping?"

"Chief!" he began excitedly. "I just found some BEAUTIFUL maples. Near Wisner Road." He started his truck, the muffler in obvious disrepair.

Dooley shouted above the racket. "Be careful in those woods. Every now and then, we get a rabid raccoon out there." He hoped Claudio heard him.

"Okay, Chief. I will! Ciao!"

Doc Reilly, whose office was a few storefronts down from the police station, had been the local, and ONLY, physician in Kirtland for over fifty years.

Everyone went to ol' Doc Reilly, and, although he was getting on in years, was as sharp as he was when he first began his practice. Even though he recently retired (*taking a little break*, he liked to say), he still came around regularly. He stood in the doorway of the office and watched the amusing interaction between Chief Dooley and Claudio as he unwrapped his trademark butterscotch hard candy, expertly popping one into his mouth. He smiled, catching Dooley's eye. "Mornin', Doc" Dooley called, giving a little salute, the tiny bottle of maple syrup still in his hand, as Doc Reilly waved back. That's when he noticed the label on the bottle:

'M. A. Y. P. E. L.'

Dooley chuckled, and, to himself, muttered, "Two thousand bottles, huh? That's a damn shame."

He started the cruiser and drove off.

Just down the block, Peter Walls, top-rated newspaper reporter in the area, stepped out of the white and blue doors of the main office of The Kirtland Stinger. Walls had recently earned some notoriety when one of his reports led to a federal investigation of some local political figures, resulting in indictments and prison terms. Today's assignment was a little less fraught with 'danger' or intrigue; he'll be interviewing the football coach of Kirtland High School. It was a good excuse to hang out with an old friend, too, Walls thought, as he stood by the curb next to his car, debating as to whether to drive or walk.

Kirtland High School wasn't that far away, and he DID need the exercise.

He unlocked his car, slid into the driver's seat, and headed off to the school.

Across town, Stan McClendon, the local go-to guy when it came to hauling big loads of anything, whether it was mattresses, landscaping material, or anything that was bulk, climbed into his rig and headed out. He had secured a good-paying haul for some of the local energy suppliers, picking up twenty tanks of propane from a supplier in Cincinnati and bringing them back to Kirtland. He had consolidated three pick-up and deliveries into one trip, making the same money but working one third as hard. Work smart, not hard his father had taught him, and he lived his life that way, owning his own truck and being his own boss.

Pulling himself into the cab of his rig, he waved to his wife as she stepped out of their house, blew a kiss to his five-year-old daughter and turned on the radio, which was going to be his driving companion for at least the next ten hours, traffic conditions permitting. At least I have the next three days to spend with my family, he thought, a big smile washing over his face.

CHAPTER THREE

As Walls pulled into the parking lot of the school, he thought about how things had changed over the years. When he went to school, kids would actually hang out together, play Frisbee, toss balls around, be ACTIVE when not in class. As he stepped out of his car and walked up to the door of the school, he shook his head as ninety-five percent of the students he passed had their faces buried in cell phones, thumbs dancing over the keypads with pinpoint accuracy, as they texted a person not three feet away. Modern technology, he thought, as he checked his cell phone before going inside. He smiled at the irony.

He walked down the hall to the doors marked 'Metal Shop', where he was set to interview the school's head football coach, Mac Gordon, who also happened to be the metal shop teacher. The class was bustling with activity, the noise from machines and the sparking of torches was an industrial symphony, accented by steam from red hot metal pieces being dipped into water. Mac sat at his old desk, probably as old as the school (and PROBABLY built by the first metal shop class!), staring out over the classroom. His eyes scanned the room, where students in gloves and masks worked grinders and arc welders. In actuality, Mac was lost in deep thought, completely unaware that the 'sanctity' of his classroom had been invaded by Peter Walls.

As Walls walked through the sounds of metal on metal, he smiled as he got closer to the front of the classroom, where Mac was perched. "Hello, Mac", he said when he thought he was close enough. When he got no response, he walked right up to him, leaned in close and once again said, "Hello, Mac."

Startled out of his meditative-like trance, Mac turned and smirked, almost ashamed that he had been caught 'napping,' although napping was the farthest thing from his mind.

"Aw, shoot, Pete", Mac said, almost coyly. "I forgot you were coming today." He stood and extended his hand, his bear-like 'paw' gripping Walls' hand like a vise.

Peter looked at Mac, then around the classroom and asked, "Bad time?" He understood Mac's busy schedule and was always willing to accommodate.

Mac was quick to respond, sensing Walls' anticipation. "Well, Doc Reilly's coming to give the team hernia exams in a bit." With THAT bit of information, Peter Walls involuntarily tightened his legs, remembering when HE had to endure a similar fate. "But, nah! You're fine."

Just as Peter's thigh muscles began to loosen, the final school bell of the day rang. Mac stood and walked to the door as the students piled out. This is something he had always done, ever since he began his tenure as metal shop teacher and head coach. It kept him on a more personal level with the students, and they respected him for it. As students walked by, most of them saying 'good byes' or waving to him, Mac singled out 16-year-old sophomore Kim, and took a step closer to her. She looked around, almost as if she didn't want the other kids to see Mac talking to her.

"Great work today, Kim," he said with a smile. "The bike looks gnarly." The word 'gnarly' seemed strange coming from the lips of someone as old as Mac Gordon—although he was only in his mid-forties—but Kim shot him a look that clearly read 'you're SUCH a dork'.

He smiled at her as she walked by, then leaned in to Peter and whispered, "She's my best student." Any other person would have taken that the wrong way, but Walls knew Mac and Mac ALWAYS treated his students with respect.

"She's making a bike!" Mac continued. " A BIKE!" Peter saw the excitement in Mac's face. Most kids these days could barely thread a needle, but here was a girl, sixteen years old, building a functioning means of transportation. Mac Gordon's chest practically swelled with pride.

That look faded as Mac's arm shot out in front of another one of his students. Dressed as if he was on his way to a Marilyn Manson concert, Blake Logan looked ominous in a long black trench coat and dark sunglasses. He stopped abruptly and turned his head toward Mac, his expression almost unreadable because of the glasses.

"Hang on, Blake," Mac said, looking into his reflexion in those glasses. "I noticed you spent a lot of time in the welding room." Blake didn't flinch or blink, not that a blink would have been noticed. The eye-to-glasses contact continued for several seconds, almost like some sort of Mexican stand-off.

"Cough it up, Blake," Mac said, breaking the silence. "You know I can't let you leave with it." The stand-off lasted another fifteen seconds, with Blake saying nothing and Mac's smile growing. Peter was getting nervous when, finally, Blake opened his trench coat, revealing one of the longest, most ornate swords he had ever seen up close. It was obvious that Mac was also impressed, as Blake reluctantly pulled the sword from inside the coat and handed it to Mac.

"Wow!" said Mac, rotating the sword in his hands, examining the fine workmanship. "Now THAT is beautiful work, Blake." He lowered the blade and looked at Blake. "Too bad no one will ever see it." Blake began to hang his head. "However," Mac continued, "congratulations on the 'A'."

Mac and Peter watched as Blake sulked his way down the hall. Examining the sword once more, and smiling at the detail and balance, Mac walked over to a pad-locked locker and opened it. There were various make-shift weapons safely tucked away, with some that were obviously precursors to this fine piece, probably also fashioned by Blake. Mac very carefully set the sword into a little niche in the corner of the locker.

Peter approached, after watching Blake leave. "What is he?" asked Peter, his head glancing back. "A freak?"

Mac almost flinched with the word, his expression becoming almost cold and stone-like. He was very protective of his students, knowing there was

19

potential in each one of them. They were HIS kids, and he didn't like when others spoke ill of them. "He's 'unique', Peter," Mac said, almost condescending. "We respect our students around here."

With that, he closed and locked the 'weapons storage' locker and walked toward the door, putting his hand on Peter's shoulder, giving him a gentle nudge. "C'mon. Let's head out to practice", and they both left the building toward the field.

CHAPTER FOUR

After bestowing his gift to Chief Dooley, Claudio drove to his home and emptied the morning's maple—or in Claudio's case, MAYPEL—into larger vats for processing. His family back in Italy originally raised an eyebrow and, in some instances, vocally opposed his choice of career change. Claudio didn't mind their reservations., Even though he did come from a long line of wine makers, in his opinion, he was still creating something that his family name could be proudly associated with. He set the empty pails into the back of his pick-up and headed back to his 'gold mine' at Wisner Woods.

As he drove along, he had his radio tuned to a local Top 40 station, and he sang along—loud enough that folks that he passed along the road turned and smiled. Every song that played became a similar-sounding Italian love song to Claudio's ears and anyone who was within earshot of this 'sing-along' was in for SOME kind of treat. The go-to song was usually Volare, whether the tune on the radio was Ariana Grande or Maroon 5, or, if he happened to change stations, Dean Martin actually singing Volare! Claudio loved America, especially Ohio.

As he reached Wisner Woods, Claudio pulled up the long, un-manicured driveway of the old Crowe estate and pulled over to the side. This was unnecessary, since no one ever went up to that area.

He hopped out of his pick-up and grabbed as many pails from the back as he could carry.

He had already strapped on his 'utility belt', as he liked to call it (Claudio LOVED the old Batman television series), which had his tools—a large hammer and his hollowed spikes that he used to drive into the maple trees to draw sap. Metal hitting metal clanked out the rhythm to yet another Italian love song, as Claudio happily walked through the woods, singing.

As he walked up to a large, untapped tree, Claudio shifted uncomfortably. He had consumed around four bottles of water and three big glasses of iced tea before he left his house, and another two bottles of water on the drive to Wisner Road. Something other than a maple tree needed to be tapped.

Claudio smiled, albeit uncomfortably, and continued singing. "Ohhhh! All this-a singing to the tree," he began, "make-a Claudio wanna pee-pee!"

As he reached down to undo his pants and relieve himself, he quickly stopped. He raised his gloved hand to his face, smiling defiantly, as if the maple-soaked glove challenged him—and lost.

"Ah-ah!" he said to his opponent. "Sticky glove." He put the glove to his mouth, and, one finger at a time, pulled it from his hand using his teeth, until he was able to shake it off.

Claudio continued to sing while he 'took care of business.' When he was finished, he gazed out upon the vast landscape of the once-grand Crowe estate. This abandoned land was now Claudio's personal liquid gold mine.

Unbeknown to the immigrant, a wet hand rose from the very ground that he had just 'watered!' The hand quickly disappeared back into the earth.

Suddenly, Claudio heard a growl.

He quickly turned but saw nothing. "Maybe it just-a my imagination", he said to the untapped tree, as he pulled a spike from his belt and began to hammer it into that same tree.

There was rustling behind Claudio, as the ground lifted again, followed by a guttural snarl. This time, Claudio turned in time to see the ground move back. He lifted his hammer, challenging his unseen visitor. No creature, big or small (preferably SMALL, thought Claudio) was going to take any of his fortune from him. Not without a fight.

"Hey! You raccoons-a come for my syrup, eh?" Claudio was ready to defend his maple 'squatters rights'. He crouched slightly, and cautiously walked toward the sound, around two feet from where he thought he saw movement, and where he had just relieved himself. I mark-a YOUR territory, he thought, smiling.

He didn't notice the patch of ground BEHIND him shift slightly as he walked.

When he reached the spot, he reached down and poked at the ground with the end of his hammer. Suddenly, the patch of ground that had shifted behind him rose up, as if a trap door had sprung open, and two dirt-covered hands—LARGE hands—shot out from the opening and grabbed Claudio by the ankles. He screamed and began flailing his arms about, swinging his hammer uselessly above his head, knocking one of his taps out of a tree, as he fell to the ground, hitting his head.

Slightly dazed, Claudio tried to fight off whatever is pulling him toward the hole in the ground. The more he struggled, the tighter the grip on his ankles became.

Claudio's hat fell from his head. He frantically grabbed onto a tree to stop himself from being pulled any further. His sap-soaked glove stuck to the tree but that did not stop his hand from leaving the glove, continuing into the ground with the rest of the body that the hand was attached to.. The last thing Claudio saw before being pulled underground and dirt filled his eyes was the last tree that he tapped.

A flock of birds rose from the trees as a horrible growl followed by muffled screams were heard from underground

A raccoon emerged from a nearby bush, slowly making its way to where Claudio had urinated, and sniffed the ground. It jumped back suddenly when another dirty hand, slightly smaller than those that grabbed Claudio, reached out of the first hole and quickly snatched Claudio's hat, and, just as quickly, disappeared back into the ground.

The sticky glove was all that remained.

CHAPTER FIVE

Peter and Mac walked along the fence line outside the school, making their way to the opening that led to the football field. Kirtland had won last year's state championship with a perfect season and, surprisingly enough, no injuries. Nick Morelli, assistant coach to Mac, wanted another perfect year, so he was working the team hard.

Peter watched the players run through their moves, Morelli barking out instructions like a wannabe drill Sargent. "What do you think sets your kids apart from the rest and how do you think it affects the game?" he asked Mac as they walked.

The sound of two football players colliding helmet to helmet created an explosive, crashing sound, startling both Mac and Peter. Assistant coach Morelli wasted no time in his 'rebuttal'. "C'mon, guys!" he yelled at the boys. "Rule. Number ONE: ALWAYS protect your head!"

Mac turned his attention from the action on the field back to Peter, who was also just turning back to the conversation. "Heart," the coach said. said. "Everybody's got one."

The head coach looked out onto the field, then back at Peter. "It just depends on how much of it you use on the field."

Peter glanced down at his little digital recorder, making sure it was still on. Mac was ALWAYS great with quotes and he didn't want to miss a single syllable. "If you want to be good at anything," Mac continued, "your heart has to be in it."

Perfect quote, Peter thought.

Mac continued. "I teach all my kids that and I try live that way myself." Without looking, Peter knew that Mac was full of pride in his team, and knew that if they listened to him and learned by example, they would make something of themselves outside of school.

Walls nodded. "Hmmmm. Interesting." He decided to dig a little and find out what Mac had in mind for the team this year. "Mac, last year your team won the state championship," he began. "Is there any way you can duplicate last year's perfect season?"

Mac Gordon's eyes never left the playing field. "I think so", he replied. We have a lot of guys back, so I would say our chances are pretty good." That special sense of proud was evident when he spoke of his 'guys'. Mac Gordon loved his job.

Walls saw the look, and quickly asked, "So you're guaranteeing back to back state championships?"

Mac's attention turned to Peter. Almost annoyed with the question, he turned and faced Peter. "No," he said sternly. "And you better not print that." One thing that Mac Gordon disliked about reporters is their presumptions. Peter Walls was skating on thin ice.

"But you said—", he began, but was quickly cut off.

"I said 'I THINK so'," Mac retorted. Another thing he hated was people putting words into his mouth. Mac Gordon said what he meant. "That's not a guarantee. It's a long season." He looked at Peter, and then back to the team. "Things happen. Players get hurt."

As he finished making his point, they witnessed the quarterback mishandle a snap, causing a fumble.

"Look," Mac continued. "If you ask me if I'm confident with our chances this year, I'll say yes." Making sure his point is understood, he turned and intensely looked Peter Walls directly in the eye, almost causing Peter to take a step back, then again, looked back onto the playing field. "But I can't guarantee that."

Peter Walls, sports reporter, seemed satisfied with Mac's 'dissertation'. "Fair enough, coach."

Now it was Peter Walls, the 'human interest' who took over. "On another note", he began. "Last season, your son John was named first team All-Ohio quarterback." Mac turned and looked at Peter, wondering where this line of questions was going. "He received several division one scholarship offers, yet I haven't seen his name pop up at any colleges yet. Why isn't he playing anywhere?"

Mac's face turned stern. When it came to the topic of his son, he tried to keep himself separated from it. He remembered his own father, who would boast about Mac, making promises to family and friends that Mac would do this and Mac would do that, and when Mac didn't, his father would get upset, and usually took it out on him.

As he is about to answer Peter, Mac saw the quarterback get creamed—head on—by a linebacker.

He began to hurriedly walk away. "You'll have to ask Johnny about that. Excuse me."

He broke into a sprint toward his quarterback. "Billy!" he yelled as he ran. "What the hell are you doing?" He directed his attention to Morelli. "Coach Morelli! What's rule number one?"

Coach Morelli didn't like to be called out on anything, especially when it came to quoting 'rule number one'. "I keep telling them, Coach. Always protect your head." Morelli knew what Mac was about to do, so he quickly intervened. "Mac", he said quietly so the rest of the team wouldn't hear. "Let's not repeat last year." As Mac seemed to settle down a little, Morelli added, "Just wanted to let you know Doc Reilly is here."

Mac nodded, thankful that Morelli knew the right thing to say. "Ol' Doc's here." He smiled and turned. "Okay." Mac motioned to Joe, the teams water boy. 'Water BOY' didn't exactly fit Joe's look, since Joe was in his mid-forties. To be kind, Joe was 'slow', but he had a huge heart. "Hey, Joe!" called Mac.

Joe turned and smiled, waving back as if he hadn't seen Coach Gordon in months. "Yes, Coach?" Joe began running over to where Mac and Coach Morelli were.

Mac smiled as Joe got closer. Usually, jocks were idiots and abused those in Joe's condition, but his boys were all respectful, which, Mac knew, came from proper teaching and discipline. "Get the team lined up in the gym. Doc Reilly's here for the ol' 'turn and cough' test."

Joe was always happy when Coach Gordon entrusted him to do something for the team. It made him feel as if he was part of that team, too. "Okay, coach," he replied happily, and turned toward the team on the field. Cupping his hands around his mouth, he shouted, "You heard the Coach, guys! Everybody in the gym so Doc can grab your nuts." *Joe has a way with words*, thought Mac, as he smiled and look at Morelli, who was thinking the same thing.

Mac turned and glanced at Peter, who was noodling with his recorder. "What took that old geezer so long to get here?" he asked Morelli.

Morelli smiled and kicked at the ground. "He's not as old as he used to be," he said with a grin.

Confused, Mac said, "What the hell does that mean?"

Realizing that Mac hadn't heard the 'news' yet, he continued his teasing. "He's also not as much of a 'he' as he used to be."

Doctor Susan Reilly stood outside the locker room doors, sucking on a piece of hard candy—butterscotch candy, in fact, which was old Doc Reilly's trademark, never being seen without a pocketful of them since he began his practice over fifty years ago. All of the boys—and even some of the girls—looked over at YOUNG Doc Reilly, as she looked around the hall, as if waiting for someone—which she was. She was in her mid-thirties, easily not looking a day over twenty-five, and very attractive; not exactly the type of woman with the title 'doctor' in front of her name. She had a sassy professionalism about her, which caused Mac Gordon to literally slow down as he approached her, taking in every inch of her.

He realized he was ogling. Coach Morelli and Peter Walls, flanking Mac, also slowed, only because Mac did. They both turned and looked at him, grinning like jack o' lanterns. She noticed the three men approaching and directed her attention toward them, smiling and stepping closer. She glanced at Mac's shirt, which read 'Coach Gordon', and walked right up to him, smiling. "Coach Gordon?," she said. "I'm Doctor Reilly."

Mac went from 'slow' to 'stop', standing stone-faced and speechless. After what seemed like an uncomfortable eternity, Coach Morelli cleared his throat and gave Mac a little nudge with his elbow. Mac snapped out of his dream world, suddenly realizing that he was acting like one of his freshmen students. "I'm sorry", he stammered. "Did you say Doctor REILLY?"

Understanding his confusion, Susan smiled and nodded. "That's me", she said reassuringly.

Mac Gordon finally regained his professional composure. "Wow", he said. "The last time we met, you were fifty years older, about eighty pounds heavier, and...", he paused when he saw Susan Reilly coyly look down and smile. "What happened to your mustache?"

"No one told you my grandfather retired, did they?" she asked, obviously knowing the answer.

"Nope," replied Mac, taking in a deep breath and pumping out his chest, "and I'm a pretty healthy guy so I haven't had the need to see him."

She extends her hand in greeting. "Doctor Susan Reilly, at your service." She said, as Mac shook her hand, holding it for a little longer than usual. I've taken over my grandfather's practice."

As Mac let go of Susan's hand, he looked at Peter and Morelli, and back to her. "Do you know why you're here?" he asked, almost embarrassed.

Susan smiled again. *She has the prettiest smile*, Mac thought. She sensed Mac Gordon's discomfort. "Yes", she said. "Every year, my grandfather performed the boys' hernia exams." She looked at Peter and Morelli, and then back at Mac. "Why do YOU think I'm here?"

Caught off guard, Mac was at a loss for words. "I... I just... uh..."

Susan Reilly suddenly became DOCTOR Susan Reilly, more as a show for the two who were flanking Coach Gordon. "Coach", she said in an ultra-professional voice. "Are you uncomfortable with a *woman* administering that test?"

She began to lay it on thick, as Peter Walls, gossip reporter, began jotting notes down. *This is getting juicy*, he thought.

Mac turned and saw Peter's smirk and the way he gingerly was taking notes. "Okay, Peter", he said, placing his hand on Susan's back, and escorting her toward the gymnasium. "This interview is OVER." They walk into the gym, and the doors swing shut behind them, leaving Peter on the outside, staring at doors. he turns toward Coach Morelli, who is looking at him, smirking.

It couldn't get much worse, thought Mac, as he and the young Doc Reilly walked into the gym, and all eyes—young, male, TEENAGE eyes—turned toward them. *Oh, boy*, he almost said aloud, sighing deeply instead.

He stopped and gently tugged at Susan's arm. "Look, I mean…", he whispered. *What's wrong with me?*, he thought. *I can't string five words together to make a sentence.* "You know, you're a doctor, and… Well, you know, I'd have no problem if you'd check ME out."

Looking away, he muttered, "Wow, now THAT came out creepy." He looked back at her. "Sorry. I mean… what I meant to say is… Okay, look." *I'm REALLY sounding like an idiot*, he thought, hoping that he didn't say THAT out loud. He regained some composure—and what was left of his dignity—and continued. "These are teenage boys, some of 'em right off the farm, and they can be a little, well, 'immature'. So, it MIGHT be better if, uh…"

"If a male doctor gave the test", Susan said, completing his sentence. "Wow, Coach. Are you aiming for sexism or chivalry?" Susan was pushing his buttons.

Mac, realizing he WAS sounding like an idiot, took a deep breath. "Chivalry, I hope." He looked at her and smiled. "But some people say chivalry *is* sexism. So I'm probably screwed either way."

Susan looked back at Mac and said, "I spent six years in med school. I've done a hernia exam before, so…"

Mac interrupted. "I'm not talking about a hernia EXAM. I'm talking about hernia EXAMS—plural." He gestured to the waiting group of testosterone-filled boys. "They stand in a row. That's a lot of hormones and you're h… uh, an attractive woman, and…"

Susan looked right into Mac's face and saw him begin to become a crimson hue. "Coach", she said. "Were you about to call me 'hot'?"

Mac looked down, fully beet red at this point.

"I don't know if I should be more worried about the boys or you!" She turned and took a few steps toward the boys, looking over her shoulder at Mac. "Plus they've already seen me. They'd riot if you sent me away."

It was time for Mac to turn the conversation around to where HE was in control, AND more comfortable. "Wait," he began. "Six years? I thought med school was eight years." *Much better.*

Susan had anticipated the question. "It IS, if you're not a genius."

Coach Mac Gordon stood there, his shoulders dropping in defeat. Morelli saw the look on poor Mac's face and went in for the save, handing him the clipboard with the team roster. Mac looked at Morelli, who gave him a knowing wink, and walked over to the current Doc Reilly, and handed her the clipboard. "Okay. Have at it," and then added as he turned to the team, "genius." He blew his whistle and addressed the team. "Alright, guys. Line up according to number. Doc Reilly's here," pointing to Susan.

The team lined up court side, somewhat confused by the sight of the current Doc Reilly. Some stood silently, some began blushing, and some seemed to get excited at the thought of a hot doctor fondling their nads.

Craig Brewer and Timothy Munczenski were toward the end of the line. Craig couldn't take his eyes off Susan. "Whoa! That must be the NEW Doc Reilly," he said, giving Tim a conspiratorial nudge.

"New AND improved," added Tim. "Sweeeet!" A quick glare from Mac stifled any further remarks.

As Mac walked Susan across the room to the start of the line, he made sure that his team heard what he was saying. "Okay, Doc. You can take it from here." He turned toward Joe and Morelli. "If you need anything, I'll be over there, talking to my staff." As the words were leaving his lips, the team erupted in giggles. Even Morelli couldn't control a chuckle or two. It dawned on Mac what the jocularity was about and, once again, he flushed with redness. "I mean," he began, "I meant MY ASSISTANT COACHES." He scowled at the team, and threw a quick silent *screw you* to Morelli. "Shut up, you guys! NOW!" As the team quieted down, Mac walked over to Coach Morelli and Joe.

"How'd THAT work for ya?" joked Morelli.

Still scowling, Mac said, "Shut up, smart ass." He watched as Susan looked over the clipboard, keeping a close eye on how the boys were treating her, and making sure they wouldn't embarrass him or themselves. *They would get used to her in time,* he thought, as she approached her first 'victim'.

Now in full 'doctor' mode, Susan walked up to the first boy in the line. "Your name is Ron Viderval?" she asked, looking up from the clipboard. The boy nodded, looking to the rest of the team. "Please lower your shorts." As she said this, Ron's face broke into a huge Cheshire Cat-like grin, as the rest of the team erupted in laughter.

Coach Gordon would not have any of this. "Cut the crap, you guys!" He glares at Ron. "Ron!" He makes a 'go ahead' motion with his head as the commotion subsides.

Susan, or now, Doctor Reilly, stared down the team, glancing at each one of them, and they all grew quiet. She stepped directly in front of Ron, close enough that Ron began to feel uncomfortable. He slid his shorts down, and, as he stood, could not look the doctor in the eyes. "Turn your head and cough," she said, her voice practically booming, as she grabbed Ron's testicles, giving them a firm squeeze. Ron's wince was noticeable. It would seem that the *Susan* part of Doc Reilly wanted to prove a point, and the point was received. "Very good," she said, and allowed Ron to lift his shorts back up.

Further down the line, Craig and Timothy continued joking, not concerned that their testicles may share a similar fate as their teammate. "She's so much better than old Doc Reilly," Tim said, as he watched her examine the next boy in line.

Craig nodded. "Yeah," he said with a grin, and then, feigning thoughtful contemplation, added, "I always felt like he held on to my balls way longer than he needed to." They both tried to hide their laughter.

Continuing the mood of obnoxious thoughtfulness, Tim added, "What bothered me is he would look right into your eyes while he did it." This time they laughed a little too loud, which got them a stern look from both Mac and Coach Morelli. The stern look from both coaches became a look of mild amusement.

The next player in line for examination was Garrett Fletcher, affectionately known as 'Rhino'. Standing at 6 feet, 2 inches tall, Garrett was the biggest member of the team - in more ways than one. His nickname did not come from his size, nor did it come from his tackling ability. As Doc Reilly walked up to him, he lowered his shorts and then stood back up, with a proud look plastered across his face. As Susan reached out to do her job, she was slightly startled as something resembling a rhinoceros horn greeted her. Someone snickered, while someone else whispered, "Two hands", but the doctor maintained her composure and continued the exam.

"Whoa! She's good," Morelli whispered to Mac. "She didn't even flinch."

Joe, not exactly one to hold back his thoughts, and who didn't completely grasp the concept of 'quiet', piped in. "He's got a big dong."

Mac just shook his head.

Maintaining her air of professionalism, Dr. Reilly politely asked Garrett, "Would you mind, uh, moving that out of the way?" With that proud look still on his face, he obligingly 'hoisted' his manhood out of her way as she maneuvered her hand around it. "Thank you," she said, and cupped his testicles. "Now turn your head and cough."

As the coaches watched, Morelli leaned in to Mac and whispered, "You know, Mac. We could PROBABLY sneak you in at the end there." Mac wasn't in the mood at the moment, as Susan continued down the line. She had just finished with Don Fenton, and next up was Timothy Munczenski.

"Morelli," Mac said sternly. "Not from YOU. Not today." Morelli knew better than to question Mac, especially when he didn't leave things open for discussion.

Susan was jotting down notes on her clipboard as she stepped up to Tim. "Timothy Mun..." She was having trouble pronouncing his name.

"Munczenski, ma'am," he said.

"Thank you, Timothy." She stopped writing and looked at the boy. "Okay, drop your shorts." There was a short pause, but Tim made no effort to oblige. He seemed nervous, slightly embarrassed even. "It's okay," Susan said reassuringly. "I've done this before." As Tim reluctantly lowered his shorts and stood, Susan looked down—and quickly back up! At this point, both Timothy Munczenski AND Dr. Susan Reilly were red-faced.

Not missing a beat, Coach Morelli brought the situation WAY out into the open. "Hey, Coach. Check out Munczenski."

Both Mac and Joe looked over at Susan and Tim. Tim's penis was standing at full attention. "Munczenski, are you kidding me?!" Mac *really* hoped that Joe wouldn't throw his two cents in.

Susan was sympathetic. "Coach, it's fine. Really…", but it was too late. The Coach stormed over to them, and pointed across court.

"Walk it off, Munczenski!" Mac barked, as Timothy ran away. Susan's next patient was another one of the jokers and Tim's partner in crime, Craig Brewer, who could barely contain his laughter, all at his friend's expense. "Don't you even smile, Craig," Mac warned. "I swear to God…" Craig looked as if he was about to explode, as Coach Gordon stared right at him.

Fortunately for Craig, just as he was about to unleash gales of laughter, the gym door burst open with a loud BANG, as Mr. Doug Brady, another shop teacher, popped in. "Hey, Coach," he said. "They said you were in here. Sorry to bother."

Mac trotted over to Doug, and said quietly, "Not the best time."

Not caring that he was interrupting, he continued. "No, quick reminder. Tiki party is this Saturday!" As if he was revealing the most important news, he repeated, "THIS Saturday!" He turned his head and, for the first time, noticed Susan. His eyes widened. "Oh! Who's the fox?"

He ran his fingers over his lips and added: "Mind if I get in line?"

Mac shot him a smack on the arm. Doug turned just in time to see Tim running by, the lad still with his erection making his shorts stick out like a pup tent. Coach Morelli was running behind him, yelling like some kind of drill sergeant.

"What are you teaching these kids?" asked Doug Brady, a puzzled look on his face.

CHAPTER SIX

After one of the craziest days he's ever had at work, Mac Gordon breathed a deep sigh of relief as he pulled into his driveway. *Remind me to NEVER take ANYTHING for granted*, he thought to himself. A NEW Doc Reilly, FEMALE, no less. He glanced to the side of the house, noticing that the garbage had not been brought down to the curb. *A father's work is never done*.

He got out of the car and drug the two garbage bins to the curb. Brushing off his hands, he headed into the house.

As he closed the door behind him, he breathed a DEEPER sigh, more to inhale the scent of 'home' than anything else. As he slowly exhaled, he heard commotion in the kitchen.

His first thought was burglar, until he looked through the kitchen doorway and saw trash littered throughout the kitchen, followed by an odd growling.

Mac shook his head. "Cujo!" he shouted, and was greeted with the sound of more growling and trash being knocked about. "CUJO!" he yelled louder. Silence and then the sound of tiny footsteps coming closer. Suddenly Cujo came running through the door. The guardian of the family, all eleven pounds of Chihuahua, pranced into the room. a far cry from the Cujo in the Stephen King novel and movie.

"Look at the mess you've made," he said, bending over, both hands fluffing the dog's head. Cujo blinked at Mac and then quickly turned and ran back into the kitchen, probably to continue his mischief-making.

As he watched the tiny excuse of a dog run off, Mac turned and looked toward the stairs with a scowl. He glanced down at his watch—5:04 p.m.—and grimaced as he stormed up the steps and down the hall to his son's bedroom.

Once again, he took a deep breath (*three within five minutes*, he thought) and politely knocked on the door. No answer. He knocked again, a bit louder and called, "Johnny!" No answer. "Johnny!" No answer. *Screw privacy*, he thought, and shouldered his way into the room.

The first thing that went through Mac's mind was *disgusting*, followed by *whose kid IS this*, as he maneuvered his way around a maze of dirty clothes and assorted magazines and video games. There were clothes strewn even on the ceiling fixture.

He WAS slightly amused at the pyramid, no, wait, THREE pyramids, made from empty beer cans. Hidden amidst the debris was a bed and lying across the bed, fully clothed and wearing ear buds was Johnny Gordon, fast asleep, with music blasting into his head.

Mac walked over to the bed that almost hid his son. "Johnny," he said. "Johnny, get up. Johnny!" Oblivious to his father's presence, Johnny shifted slightly. Mac reached down and unceremoniously yanked ear buds from Johnny's head, startling him awake by the sudden silence.

"I'm up! I'm up," he said groggily. His eyes began to droop.

"It's five o'clock," barked Mac.

"Dad," Johnny whined. "Come on."

"In the EVENING."

"Wow. Five already," was the smug response.

"Yeah. It looks like you caught a touch of that hangover that's been going around," said Mac, as he knocked the top can from the taller beer can pyramid.

Mac was right. Johnny had been up drinking well into the night, and he had heard him clanking around in his room as he left for work that morning. "Okay, okay. Very funny." Johnny sat up and threw his feet off the bed, careful not to knock over his construction masterpiece. "I'm up, okay?"

Mac was growing less amused, not that he was amused to begin with. "So THIS is your plan instead of going to college." More of a statement of fact than a question.

"Yeah, Dad," said Johnny. "It's just for a year. Chill."

"Chill!" Mac's eyes widened. "Chill? How can I *chill*? It looks like Cheech and Chong have been living up here," he exclaimed as he gestured about the room with his hand. "Cujo tore the hell out of the kitchen!" Johnny began to giggle at the thought of that tiny excuse for a dog creating havoc, but saw the look in his father's eyes. "I need you to clean it up." As Johnny was about to protest, Mac cut him off. "NOW!"

Johnny had spent a good part of the next hour cleaning the mess Cujo had blessed them with . He looked at the tiny dog and exclaimed: "How the hell could YOU make a mess like THIS?" He pointed to two full bags of trash.

Mac walked in just as Johnny finished cleaning. As he began preparing dinner, Johnny took out the trash bags and went upstairs. He walked into his bedroom, still careful not to knock over the Great Pyramids of Kirtland, stripped off his clothes from yesterday, and went into the bathroom to shower.

Mac had chicken thawed and was preparing his famous chicken cutlet Parmesan. Mac enjoyed cooking, even if it was only for Johnny—and Cujo, of course.

Ever since his wife left, it's just been the two—THREE—of them, and Mac wanted the best for his son, even though he rarely showed any appreciation. It seemed Johnny blamed Mac for his mother leaving, *but who could blame him*, Mac thought. Gone, without even leaving a note or calling to check on him. Mac was bitter and upset that she left, but he couldn't imagine how Johnny felt.

About forty minutes later, Mac was pulling the chicken out from the oven, as Johnny, freshly showered and in clean clothes, came bounding down the stairs and headed straight for the door. Still sporting oven mitts, he went to the kitchen doorway just as Johnny was opening the front door. "Where are you going?"

"Out with Ziggy and Tony," replied Johnny. He began to hurry now that he had been caught.

"I just finished making supper."

Johnny was out the door and closing it as he said, "Well, thank you, honey." And just like that, he was gone.

Mac heard Johnny's van start up, pull out of the driveway and roar down the road.

He felt more alone than he had in a long time.

CHAPTER SEVEN

The old Brown Chevy van rumbled down the road. Johnny's friends, Ziggy and Tony, waited on a corner several blocks from the Gordon house because both both were intimidated by Mac. On more than one occasion, Mac Gordon had thrown each of the boys out of the house, so they all agreed that it would be wise to meet in a neutral location. Johnny pulled over to the curb, where Ziggy hopped into the 'shotgun' seat and Tony eagerly found his spot in front of the make-shift video 'arcade' they had set up in the back of the van. As useless as everyone thought Ziggy and Tony were, they certainly knew how to set up electronics and play video games.

Ziggy turned and watched Tony, as he shifted and grunted in front of his fantasy world of battle. Johnny glanced in his rear view mirror and just shook his head.

"So, what's up, bro?" asked Ziggy, punching Johnny in the arm. The three had been friends since they were in grade school and, no matter what, they vowed to have each other's backs.

"My old man. AGAIN," Johnny replied, flustered. Tony was lost in his own world. "He just in that 'no son of mine' mood lately—"

"Or maybe," Ziggy interrupted, "his new quarterback isn't as much fun to yell at as YOU are!"

"Shut up, asshole,"

Seeing that he was annoying Johnny, Ziggy quickly changed the subject. "Are there gonna be any chicks at this party?"

Johnny wanted to vent. "Dude, I was trying to..." He saw that his words were lost on his cohorts, so he change his topic to what was most important to his friends. "Yes, Ziggy, yes," Johnny said in a condescending tone. "It's a party. A bunch of chicks from Lake Girls Academy are having a huge blowout down by the springs." He glanced over at Ziggy, and then over his shoulder at Tony. "A bunch of babes." And then, adding with a smirk, "And a bunch of booze."

Hearing his two favorite things, Tony, not missing a shot on his game, blurted out, "Babes and booze," and, suddenly, fully focused on the game, mumbled, "Die, bitches!"

A sudden look of mild panic washed across Ziggy's face. "There's not gonna be a lot of dudes there, right?" He frantically looked back and forth between Johnny and Tony. Johnny shook his head.

"No dudes."

Ziggy, undaunted in his panic, and probably slightly paranoid from the cannabis of which he had just partaken, continued. "Cause I don't want to be at a sword fest. You know. A sausage party."

"No sword fest," Johnny replied.

"I'm not down with the sword."

"No sword." Johnny was equally amused and annoyed.

"Sword sucks."

Johnny could not resist. "Sucking the sword."

Ziggy's head spun so fast at Johnny's seriously-delivered remark that he almost got whiplash. "No, I'm not sucking a sword."

From the back, Tony piped in. "Enough already with the sword." His attention never left the screen throughout Johnny and Ziggy's 'swordplay'. "I'm trying to focus."

Johnny, ever the straight man, threw in his opinion. "Quiet back there!"

"Damn it," Tony erupted.

Concerned, Johnny asked, "What?"

"It just changed my weapon."

Oh, such an emergency, Johnny thought.

Ziggy couldn't resist. "Did it change... to a *sword*?"

Pausing his game and climbing from his seat, Tony reached over the passenger's seat and began to choke Ziggy with one arm, while smacking him about the head with the other.

"That's it!" Johnny snapped into referee mode and began whacking Tony on the head with an empty plastic soda bottle. *What the hell is a soda bottle doing in here?*, he asked himself.

In his best lion tamer voice, Johnny accented his hits to Tony head with, "Get back, beast! Back!"

Ziggy and Tony calmed down, and Tony climbed back into his seat and resumed his game. Johnny noticed a look of slight panic on Ziggy's face as his breathing slowed down.

"One of these days," Ziggy began as Johnny looked at him, "he's really gonna strangle me—" But before he could finish his sentence, Ziggy's eyes widened in surprised shock as he saw something dart out from the side of the road and into the path of the van, right in the middle of the headlights.

"LOOK OUT!" Ziggy shouted. Johnny turned his head in time to see someone in the road. He slammed down hard on the brakes, but it was too late. The van plowed into what seemed to be a child. The three of them lurched forward as the van screeched to a halt, Tony's head smacking into the back of Ziggy's seat.

"Oh, shit!" Johnny said. "Oh, SHIT!"

Ziggy shook his head, as if clearing his thoughts. "Dude!" was all he could say.

From the floor of the back, Tony said, "What the hell was that? What did you hit?"

Still a bit paranoid, a wild-eyed Ziggy got right into Johnny's face. "Let's get outta here!" he screamed.

Johnny, not the least bit 'enhanced', was the voice of reason. "We can't leave," he said. "C'mon man we gotta check it out," as he opened his door. Ziggy grabbed his arm.

"Are you crazy?" Ziggy retorted. "Let's go." He looked down as if in deep thought and continued. "We'll stop at a car wash on the way home!"

Johnny pulled out of Ziggy's grip and got out of the van. "It's a kid, man," he said to Tony and Ziggy. "It's a little kid. I'm going to check it out."

Undaunted, Ziggy continued his protests. "Dude, get back in here! Let's go!" Seeing that his words went unheeded, he shrugged and mumbled to himself, "He went out. Damn it." He shook his head. "He never listens."

As Ziggy straightened himself out, Tony climbed back into his seat and continued playing his video game. Ziggy decided to see for himself what happened, so he opened his door and climbed out, joining Johnny in front of the van.

Johnny stood in the middle of the road, the vans headlights shining on him as he leaned over what, at first, looked like a nine-year-old child, but with a very large, misshapen head, swollen, with eyes almost on the extreme left and right sides.

As Ziggy approached the victim and got a look, he quickly turned, choking back vomit. "What the hell is THAT?" he asked, not looking.

"I don't know," replied Johnny.

"Is it human?"

Johnny leaned in closer. "I THINK so," and then added, "barely." He moved even closer.

Ziggy, determined to be the 'voice of reason', had made up his mind. "Okay, Let's kick it into the woods and hit that car wash." He mustered some nerve, swallowed hard, and turned toward Johnny and the 'child'.

"We can't do that," Johnny protested, holding out his arm. "We have to go to the police." He looked at Ziggy. "It's a person."

Ziggy's eyes widened in shock at Johnny's insane talk. "The police?! What are you crazy?!" He tried to push past Johnny, but Johnny was firm.

"Yeah, this was an accident." He looked at the body in the road. "It could have happened to anyone." Trying to reassure a panicking Ziggy, he said smoothly, "We'll be fine."

Ziggy shook his head. "No!" he said adamantly. "No, we won't." He looked in the back, where Tony continued his game as if nothing happened. "Tony's got a bag of weed the size of my head in the car." *NOW he'll realize I'm right,* he thought.

Johnny was losing his patience. "Well, tell Tony to hide the weed in the woods and we'll come back for it or something." He bent over the body. "This is a bigger deal."

Neither one of them noticed Tony climbing out of the van and walking toward them. Hearing the last part of the conversation, he said, "Wait, why are we hiding the we—" and then he saw the body. "Whoa!" he said, taking a step back. "You hit an alien!"

Ziggy was suddenly coherent. "It's not an alien."

"How do YOU know?"

With Mr. Spock-like logic, Ziggy replied, "Because aliens don't wear Reebok's, dickhead."

Suddenly, another figure came crashing through the brush. Bloated and bug-eyed like the mutant creature in the road, this one was much larger. It saw the three boys hovering over its dead sibling, and let out a horrifying, high-pitched scream. The three threw their hands over their ears, trying to block out the noise, which was like daggers in their heads. They all turned.

"Oh, wow," said Tony. "That alien's mad."

Scared 'straight', Ziggy truly WAS the voice of reason this time. "Okay, time to go!" Looking quickly at Johnny and Tony, he repeated, "Time to GO!"

Johnny stood up and tried to console the 'mutant' that was wailing at them. "We're sorry. It was an accident."

The creature continued screaming.

"He just ran in front of the car. We didn't see him." *He's GOT to understand*, Johnny thought. "We didn't mean it." Just as Johnny was trying to explain, the woods shook, and several more of Tony's 'aliens' emerged, rushing to the side of the screamer, as it pointed to the body lying in the road.

Tony chimed in. "Are you done negotiating?" They were seriously outnumbered.

Suddenly, the bushes opened again, and a very large big-headed, bug-eyed mutant stomped out of the woods. Very, VERY large. Johnny's eyes widened, as he thought *alpha male*. They saw a hose dangling from its head, and some sort of fluid was gushing from the end of it. It saw the body in the road and the three boys surrounding it, and let out the most blood-curdling scream ever heard.

Ziggy was staring at this monstrosity as it slowly walked toward them. "Guys. Can we go now?"

Behind him, he heard two van doors slammed, and he realized his friends had abandoned him. "Guys?" He turned and ran toward the van. "Oh, CRAP!" he said as he jumped into the van.

Johnny put the van in reverse and backed up fast, tires screeching, and whipped the vehicle around, and then shifting it into DRIVE, speeding away.

Ziggy settled into his seat, turned to Johnny and glared at him. "Thanks for waiting." *Asshole.*

Johnny was too busy concentrating on the road to turn. "Sorry, man. We were too scared to say anything, so we ran."

The van sped down the road.

CHAPTER EIGHT

The giant, fluid-gushing mutant stared down at the lifeless body of the child, and suddenly looked up with rage-filled eyes focusing on the taillights of the van drove away. He looked at each one of the other 'things' that surrounded the body, and then charged down the road after the van. Trees and shrubbery were nothing but a blur as this fluid-gushing creature bolted down the road, quickly caught up to the van. The three boys were completely unaware of what was racing up behind them.

"Not an alien, huh?" Tony said. "So, Mr. Ziggy, tell me this. How many HUMANS do you know that have tubes coming out of their heads?"

Hyped up on adrenaline from almost being left behind, Ziggy turned to confront Tony. Before he could say anything, though, he glanced out of the rear window of the van, and saw the giant mutant, rocketing toward the van.

Instead of arguing with Tony, he stared out the window and said, "Look at that bitch run!" But, just before anyone else could catch a glimpse of their impending peril, the creature launched itself into the air. "Hold on," said Ziggy, in a tone most foreboding.

Suddenly they feel a loud THUD on the roof of the van, and then shuffling, as if someone was taking a walk above them.

And then silence.

After a few seconds, Tony silently spoke. "Did he fall off?" No sound. They looked around at each other, breathing a sigh of relief. They started to relax.

A dirty, LARGE fist came crashing through the roof of the van! It scratched at the air above the boys, reaching for anything that could be grabbed. Johnny swerved the van, first left and then right, side to side, trying to shake off the unwelcome invader. The fluid-gushing giant was very strong, though, and held steadfastly onto the vehicle.

As the struggle progressed, Tony began thrashing around in a fit of panic.

The big bad of weed fell to the floor of the van. Tony kicked it toward the front, right under Johnny's feet as he tried to shake the thing off.

Irritated and annoyed at his stoner friend's flailing around, but still focused on his driving, Johnny reached down, grabbed the weed, and tossed it out of the window.

"Hey!" yelled Tony, finding his own 'focus'. "What are you doing?"

"Sorry," Johnny said, almost sarcastically, considering the situation.

"Nooooo!" cried Tony. Johnny shook his head.

The beast on the roof began to squeeze itself through the hole in the roof, snapping the boys back to their current predicament. It reached in, swiping at Tony, who became trapped between the side of the van and the arm of doom.

As the fingers drew closer, Tony reached out and grabbed the nearest weapon, his trusty bong, and smashed it on the creature's arm, leaving a long sharp broken point. "Oh, shit," Tony muttered. "My bong!" He looked at the remains. "Loved that bong."

He flew into a rage at the loss of his love. "You alien piece of shit!" he screamed as drove the broken shard into the creature's forearm. Blood spurted from the creature's arm, as it reached with the other hand and yanked out the glass. Tony stared in disbelief.

"Dude," Ziggy shouted. "Slam on the brakes!"

Good idea, thought Johnny. "Hold on!" he said, as he slammed both feet onto the brake pedal, launching their attacker over the top of the van, and slamming him into the road ahead. It landed hard, and the forward momentum sent it skidding across the pavement. It lay motionless about fifty feet in front of the van. The sound of the van idling was loud in their ears.

"Is he dead?" asked Ziggy, staring at the figure in the headlights up ahead.

"He looks pretty dead to me," replied Johnny, as he too looked at the thing in the road, and then, as an afterthought, looked up at the gaping hole in the roof of his van.

"Run it over and make sure," said Ziggy.

Tony nodded, but no one saw him, and then added, "Oh, hey. Thanks for chucking my weed."

Both Johnny and Ziggy turned to Tony and, at the same time, said, "Shut up, dude." They looked at each other and smiled uncomfortably at their timing.

"We gotta go to the cops," Johnny continued. "I can't have weed in here."

Just as they were about to drive off, Tony looked out the front window. "Guys," he said, almost in a whisper. "Where's the body?"

Johnny and Ziggy turned. Tony was right. There was no body in the road where there had been one moments before! The three of them looked to the left and right of the roadway, seeing nothing but shrubs.

Johnny was the first to say something. "It must have crawled away." But he spoke too soon, as the gushing monstrosity sprang up in front of the van and jumped on the windshield. Grabbing the roof of the vehicle, the thing lashed out, kicking in the glass, spraying the boys with broken shards.

As the thing was trying to gain some footing to resume its attack, Johnny floored the gas pedal, sending the thing up and over the top of the van. The boys heard two loud thumps as the thing's body slammed into the roof before tumbling off the back, landing solidly in the road as the van sped off.

As fluid dribbled from the hose that protruded from its head, the thing snarled at the fading red taillights.

CHAPTER NINE

A fuming Coach Mac Gordon stormed into the police department. *I have to stay cool*, he thought, as his demeanor went from parental anger to dignified diplomacy. He walked up to the desk and tried his best to smile at the officer, who was sitting their reading the morning newspaper. "I'm here to pick up Johnny Gordon, please."

The officer sitting at the front desk politely stood and said, "Just one moment, sir." He picked up the phone, punching one of the intercom buttons: "Chief Dooley," he said into the phone. "Coach Mac is here."

"He's coming right out," the officer acknowledged to Mac as he hung up the phone and resumed his reading of the newspaper.

Mac's 'dignified diplomacy' received a smack in the face as he glanced at the sports section headline. 'COACH MAC GUARANTEES CHAMPION-SHIP' screamed boldly from the page.

Frowning, Coach Mac pulled his cell phone from his pocket, turned his back to the officer at the desk, and hit a number on his speed dial.

After four rings, Mac heard the voice mail greeting. "You've reached Peter Walls. You know what to do. Hit me." *I would LOVE to*, thought Mac.

After the beep, Mac, in his most polite yet angry tone, said, "Hi, Peter. Coach Mac here. You are NOT allowed at practice anymore."

He hung up just as Chief Dooley walked in, a sheepish grin plastered on his face. "Mornin', Coach," he said, still smiling. "Looks like your superstar had a heck of a night!"

Not mincing words, Mac asked, "What happened?" He almost didn't want to know.

Dooley became somewhat professional. "Johnny and his buddies were driving down Wisner Road and hit something."

"A deer?" Mac asked, hopeful.

"I don't know," replied Dooley. He shrugged. "They're telling me a crazy story that they hit some sort of freak."

"What?" Mac said, eyes widening.

"Yep," said Dooley. "Yep. Then, after they hit him, they say this freak's dad jumped on top of the van and tried to kill them." Dooley shook his head.

"A freak?"

"Yep. AND his Dad, AND brothers, AND uncles." He paused for a moment. "That's what two of them think. The third one thinks they hit an alien." He looked at Mac. "Pissed off a whole family of aliens."

Mac looked at Dooley. "What do you think?"

Avoiding any otherworldly explanations, Dooley said, "I think that van smelled like weed." He paused. "BUT, there's blood on the front of the van and the roof is pretty torn up." He thought for a second. "They mighta hit a deer and launched it on the roof. I went out to the scene, but I didn't see any carcass. I DID find some blood, though, so I know they hit SOMETHING."

Mac eyes showed their concern. "Where are the boys?" he asked.

Almost embarrassed, Dooley said, "I have them in a holding cell."

"Why?" asked Mac. "Did you arrest them?"

"No."

"Then they didn't need to be locked in a cell," Mac said, almost confrontational.

Dooley flashed Mac a challenging smile, but said, "No. No, they didn't."

"Would you get them, please?"

Dooley softened a little. "Sure, Coach." As he walked away, he turned and looked at Mac, and then continued to the holding cell. *Lesson is over, boys*, he thought with a smile.

The scene that greeted Chief Dooley as he approached the holding cell was almost straight out of a comedy. Johnny and Tony were huddled together tightly in one corner of the cell, as Ziggy was in another corner—but not alone. He was cradled in the lap of Blue Barlow. Blue was about six-foot two, two hundred twenty pounds, and, today, quite dirty and unshaven. He had been in the holding cell before the boys were placed in with him.

"I think we're alone now," he sang to Ziggy, his voice harsh. "There doesn't seem to be anyone around." Ziggy drew into himself more.

Johnny looked around the cell and then glanced at Ziggy and his 'guardian'. "This is horrible," he muttered.

Tony was equally uncomfortable. "Yeah, I know," he replied. "I don't like *Tiffany* either." Johnny looked at him and shook his head, just as Chief Dooley entered the holding cell.

"Okay, you guys," he said to them. "Time to go."

"Thank God," said Johnny, as he and Tony sprang from their bench and hurried out the cell. Ziggy, on the other hand, was still in Blue's 'loving' embrace.

"Let him go, Blue," Dooley said, nodding toward the two.

Blue loosened his hold on Ziggy, and, as Ziggy carefully backed away from him, said, "Better be good, boy, 'cause I'll be waiting."

With that, Ziggy darted out of the cell and joined his friends down the hall.

Dooley watched as the three walked through the doors, and after they had left earshot, he turned to Blue. "You scare the shit out of them?"

Blue smiled and said, "I think the little one was close to pissing himself," as Dooley tossed the cell keys to him.

"Give me five minutes and then let yourself out."

Blue caught the keys. "See you Sunday at church?"

Dooley turned and smiled. "Of course."

Tony was the first one to come out from the holding area, quickly followed by Johnny and Ziggy, who looked very pale. Mac stood next to the reception desk, his arms folded, glaring at Johnny. Johnny stepped quickly past Tony toward his father. "Dad," he began. "I know what your thinking, b—"

"You KNOW what I'm thinking!?" Mac angrily interrupted. "You KNOW what I'm thinking?" He tried to find something else to say, but was cut off by Tony as he walked by him.

"Hey, Coach. Ziggy almost got corn-holed." Mac stopped in mid-thought and looked at Tony, who added, "Oh, yeah. And we saw an alien."

Johnny just rolled his eyes and tilted his head back, knowing full well that Tony's little comment would only infuriate Mac.

Mac suddenly shifted into full 'Coach Mac' mode. "Tony," he said, practically hissing. "Wait outside."

Just as Tony ducked his head like a scolded dog, Ziggy hurried past Johnny and Mac, without so much as a glance at either of them.

Mac was just about to speak when Ziggy said, "I don't want to talk about it." He stopped and turned, just as Chief Dooley walked out of the back, trying to hide a smirk. The dispatch officer, who was on the phone, quickly stood and stopped him as he walked by.

"Excuse me, Chief," he said, holding out the phone to him. "I've got Claudio's mother on the phone here."

"Yeah, and..."

"She's saying he never came home yesterday."

Chief Dooley scowled as he looked at the three boys, and then right at Johnny. "You assholes didn't hit Claudio, did you?"

Johnny was quick to respond. "Is Claudio's a big-headed midget?!"

Dooley became flustered. "Congratulations," he said to Johnny. "You're officially retarded."

Tired of the nonsense, Mac grabbed Johnny by the arm. "Johnny, take those guys home and then get back to the house. You and I have some talking to do."

"Yeah, bet we do," Johnny muttered under his breath as he walked out with Ziggy and Tony at his heels.

Mac walked over to Chief Dooley, who was talking to the officer at the desk. "Tell her we'll look into it," he said, and then turned to Mac as he approached.

Mac looked almost defeated. "Are there any charges?" he asked.

"Not unless I find Claudio in a ditch with tire tracks across his chest."

Mac was not amused. "Well, then, until you do, leave my kid alone."

"Alright," Dooley replied. As Mac was leaving but not completely out of earshot, he heard Dooley whisper to the desk officer, "And THAT'S probably why the kid doesn't play ball any more. Can't control him." Coach Mac Gordon was about to turn and say something, but thought better.

He walked to his car and headed home, pondering the inevitable conversation.

CHAPTER TEN

After promising both Chief Dooley and Mac to only drop off Tony and Ziggy and then go straight home, Johnny carefully drove his practically-totaled van down the road, the wind blowing through the space that used to be a windshield stinging his eyes. As they drove along, they realized they were driving on the road where, just hours earlier, the 'incident' happened. They all were visibly tense, especially Johnny. Suddenly, Tony straightened up in his seat. "Stop the car," he said loudly, almost shouting above the wind noise.

Johnny cocked his head. "What?'

"Uh, no." Ziggy piped in.

Tony was insistent. He began bouncing in his seat, and then stood in the back of the van. "Stop the van. I wanna get out." His friends looked at him as if he had lost his mind.

"Are you crazy?" Ziggy said, and then turned to Johnny. "Don't stop, man." At this point, Tony had leaned over Johnny, and put his hands on his shoulders and began shaking him. Johnny had put up with enough of them both, so he slowed the van and pulled over, coming to a careful full stop. Even before the vehicle had been shifted to PARK, Tony slid open the door and jumped out, and then ran over to the driver's side.

"Come on, man," he said to Johnny. "Help me find my weed." Tony knew better at this point not to bother asking Ziggy, especially after the holding cell 'encounter'.

Johnny shook his head. "No way, man. You're on your own with this one."

Tony tried to guilt Johnny into helping by putting on the 'puppy-dog' look that usually worked when he was coming on to girls. "Those things are long gone by now," he whined, but Johnny was adamant.

"Dude, I am NOT hanging."

Ziggy joined in. "Tony," he said sternly, almost sounding like Coach Mac, which made Johnny look at him. "Get in the damn van."

"No," Tony said, pushing away from the van as Ziggy tried reaching for him over Johnny. "Fine," he said, stomping a foot like a spoiled child. "You guys go. I can be home in ten minutes from here."

Ziggy and Johnny looked at each other, each one thinking the same thing; *he's an idiot.*

As Ziggy shook his head, Johnny put the van into DRIVE and drove off, leaving Tony standing on the side of the road. Alone. As Tony watched the taillights fading, he suddenly realized how alone he really was. "Alright," he said aloud. "Let's make this snappy," and pulled out his cell phone and used the light that was on it to scour the shrubbery for his bag of weed.

"Weed," he called out as if it was his dog. "Where, oh, where are you?" He scanned the area with his cell phone light, pushing some of the larger growth out of the way. "I know I'm close." At one point, he got down on his hands and knees.

There, about two feet away, the light caught the glimmer of a plastic bag. "I KNEW I'd find you!" he said to the bag as he scrambled over to it. As he picked it up and began cradling it to his cheek, he noticed that it had been opened.

"What the heck! I had more than THIS!"

He held the bag up and shone the light on it, shaking his head, almost feeling betrayed. With grim determination, he sealed the bag and began rummaging through the bushes, searching, hoping to retrieve any stray buds that may have escaped. That's when he smelled something very familiar. He straightened himself up and sniffed the air. "That smells like," he paused and sniffed again. "That smells like weed." Another sniff. "MY weed!"

As this grand revelation took hold, the creature that attacked Johnny's van stepped out of the shadows and through the bushes. As it walked toward him, Tony noticed that it was smoking a corncob pipe. "Oh, shit," Tony muttered. "The alien bogarted my doob."

Spurts of some sort of fluid ran from the tube that was sticking out of the beast's head as it toked on the pipe and, as it blew out the smoke, let out another one of its blood-curdling scream. Tony stepped back from the sound, just as two more similar but slightly smaller *mutants* crashed through the brush, their heads turning from side to side, each eye getting a turn to glare at Tony.

One of them was wearing a flower-patterned housecoat (*Hey,* thought Tony. *My grandmother has one of those.*), and the other looked like a gymnast, only this gymnast had a mutant head.

"Uh...," Tony stammered nervously as he took a few steps back. "You guys can keep the doobie, okay?"

The two creatures looked at the big pipe-smoker, who made a motion to Tony. Tony knew what that meant.

"Screw this!" he said, and turned and ran, cutting frantically through brush and low branches. The limbs whipped at his face and any bare skin as he ran, tearing into his flesh and leaving red welts.

The two nightmarish beasts waited for a moment and looked at each other. Something that could be interpreted as a smile crossed their warped faces as they gave Tony a head start, and then they were off, crashing through the forest, chasing their prey.

The gymnast-mutant barreled through the woods as the housecoat-mutant climbed up and leaped from tree to tree like some sort of crazed large monkey. As the gymnast-mutant closed in on Tony, the housecoat-mutant grabbed a long thin tree and pulled it back, using it as some sort of slingshot. It vaulted itself through the air at Tony, just as Tony realized that he was running parallel with the road.

"Thank God," he said, as he turned hard and headed toward the roadway. "The road!"

Tony's sudden change in direction caught the housecoat-mutant by surprise. Instead of landing on Tony, it crashed face-first into the dirt, tumbling clumsily onto the path. The gymnast-mutant stopped abruptly, almost tripping over its cohort, and sneered and hissed, reprimanding the other one because of its failure to catch their prey.

***

As Tony was running for his life, Stan McClendon, tired from driving his truck for the last thirteen hours hauling propane tanks, decided to pour himself a nice hot cup of coffee. His eyes were heavy from staring at the road all day and into the night, so he shook his head, trying to clear the 'cobwebs' from his weary brain. Stan McClendon was completely unaware of the nightmare that was happening just yards away.

***

Tony barely escaped with his life as the two mutants—or, in Tony's eyes, aliens—scrambled to regroup and continue the hunt. Tony tore through the woods and saw the guardrail. *Home free!*, he thought, as he ran toward the road and jumped over the rail. He saw the headlights of a truck - Stan's truck - growing larger in the distance. He ran to the middle of the road and waved his arms frantically, trying to get the driver's attention. "Right here!" he shouted at the lights. "Right here! Help me!"

***

Stan finished pouring himself a cup of coffee and was too tired or distracted to notice the figure of Tony in the road, who was just out of the range of his headlights. Stan also did not see the huge pothole in the road!

The truck struck the deep divot, bouncing the vehicle hard, sending scalding liquid into Stan's lap, and loosening the latch on the back of the rig.

"God DAMN!" Stan shouted, as he looked down and tried to get the hot coffee out of his lap.

***

The lights were getting bigger as the truck got closer, but it wasn't slowing down. Tony continued to wave frantically as if his life depended on it—in fact his life DID depend on it—and yelled even louder than before.

"Hey!!! Slow down!" Tony screamed.

It suddenly dawned on him. "He doesn't see me," Tony said aloud and turned to get out of the truck's path. As he wheeled around to jump, the gymnast-thing and the housecoat-thing stood at the guardrail, waiting. Tony froze in fear.

***

Stan looked up just as his headlights caught Tony standing in the middle of the road. He slammed both feet onto the brake pedal, causing the truck to bounce hard and screech as rubber and asphalt fought momentum. The cargo, a full bed of propane cylinders, broke loose from the ratchet straps holding them in place and were sent flying into the road.

The speed and weight of the truck was too much; Stan couldn't get the rig stopped before hitting Tony. The boy's body was directly in the middle of the lane as the center of the grill caught Tony from waist to neck, and the windshield instantly made pudding of his face, splattering blood and bone across the entire front of the truck.

The vehicle *finally* came to a complete stop thirty-two feet later.

Stan sat in the driver's seat in complete and utter shock. The truck had stalled from the sudden stop and the windshield was tinted crimson.

Several seconds past, but it felt like hours to Stan before he began to frantically unbuckle his seat belt. He jumped from the cab of his truck and stood by the front tire. He was afraid of what he would see, of what he had done. He finally mustered enough courage to walk around to the front of the truck and saw the torn and twisted remains of what was once Tony. Stan closed his eyes tightly, but even that didn't keep the image from his mind. He grimaced and opened his eyes and stepped closer to the body. As he leaned toward the mangled form in the road, he heard something.

Rustling. In the woods. Behind him.

Stan stood up and turned quickly. *Who could be out here*, he thought. *Maybe this guy had friends with him. Maybe they could help*. Stan stared into the darkness. "Hello," he called. He moved closer to where he thought he heard the noise, eyes still straining to see something, ANYTHING. Instead he saw nothing but dark woods. He turned back to the body in the road...

... in time to see two creatures, one in a housecoat and the other looking like a gymnast, lunge at him.

The gymnast-thing grabbed Stan by the head and sank its teeth into him, while the housecoat-thing tore at his mid-section, shredding his clothes and then his flesh as if it was butter. The last thing Stan McClendon saw before his eyes were pulled from his head was flesh being torn from his body and devoured by gnashing teeth.

CHAPTER ELEVEN

He's late, Mac thought as he sat in the living room staring at the mantelpiece. He remembered when he and Johnny would proudly add pictures, plaques and trophies to the collection, each item a testament to Johnny's hard work and a sense of fair play instilled in him by Mac throughout his life. Mac was proud of Johnny, even though he hadn't shown it as of late. He looked at the photo of the three of them; Johnny, Mac, and his wife Eva, who had left them a while ago, and had never contacted them, not even a phone call to Johnny when he won the championship for Kirtland last year. Mac and Eva had their problems, but Johnny loved her, and her not keeping in touch with him wasn't right. Mac hung his head, not wanting to look at the picture of the once-happy family because of the painful memories. His thoughts returned to Johnny.

Where was he? He promised Chief Dooley and Mac that he would drop off his two friends and go straight home, especially with his van in the condition it was in. *He's lucky that he wasn't killed*, Mac thought, remembering the smashed windshield. *And how the hell did the roof get ripped open like that?* He heard the van pulling into the driveway. *Finally.*

Johnny quietly opened the door and eased his way in, not seeing Mac sitting on the couch. Mac shuffled a magazine so Johnny would know he was there. He turned, father looking at son, coach looking at the star athlete, neither one speaking for what seemed like hours. Johnny looked down as Mac spoke.

"What REALLY happened?" he asked.

After several seconds of awkward silence, Mac continued. "Dooley said he smelled weed in the van." He stood and walked toward Johnny, but not in a confrontational manner, but still severe enough to make Johnny tense. "Making up stories about hitting somebody? Because it's not funny, Johnny." He didn't bother saying *you should have known better*, but it was there.

"No," replied Johnny, looking at Mac straight in the eyes. "No, it's not, Dad." Something about the way Johnny spoke to Mac made him feel he needed to change the direction of the conversation rather than lay into him and read him the riot act. He paused and sat back down on the couch.

"Is your van okay?" he asked instead, a bit softer than the prior questioning..

Johnny's shoulders slumped as he headed toward the stairs. "I just wanna get some sleep."

Mac conceded. "Well, you better," he said, "because as soon as Smitty's opens, you're getting cleaned up." Smitty's Barber Shop was the typical small town hair cutting establishment, complete with dated photos of hairstyles that ALL looked like Moe Howard of the Three Stooges. "I'm tired of you looking like a bum."

With that being said, Johnny nodded and slowly walked up the stairs, down the hall and into his room. Mac heard the door slowly close, and listened as Johnny kicked off his shoes and plop loudly onto the bed. *He didn't even get undressed,* he thought, as he headed to his own room, knowing that this was going to be a restless night.

CHAPTER TWELVE

Morton Smith, Jr. had worked at Smitty's Barber Shop for most of his life before taking it over from the original 'Smitty', his father, Morton, Sr., when he passed away. It had been a Kirtland staple for decades, and hadn't changed much since it opened. "Hairstyles come and go," Smitty once said, "but Smitty's is here to stay."

Today was just like any other day, with Smitty trading barbs with Otis Gander, who hung out at Smitty's since it opened, never once showing any deference to the Smiths being one of the first black families in Kirtland. Otis's girth made him use one and a half of the chairs in Smitty's shop and Smitty always chided him about being 'slightly overweight', but it was always light-hearted. They were friends longer than most of the residents were alive.

"You must be crazy," Smitty was saying to Otis, as he trimmed a young customer's hair. "Gayle Sayers couldn't hold a candle to Jim Brown." He looked at the young man in the chair, making sure the cut was even, which it wasn't. "Hell. The man's seventy years old and he STILL could rush for a thousand yards." Smitty loved his football and he had an opinion about everything.

"Okay," countered Otis. "Who's the best quarterback of all time?"

"That's easy. Johnny Unitas."

Otis shook his head. Johnny U? NOW who's crazy?"

Undaunted, Smitty asked, "Who do YOU think?"

"Mean Joe Green."

It was Smitty's turn to shake his head. "Mean Joe Green didn't even PLAY quarterback, you old coot!"

"Yes he did."

Smitty's eyes popped open in amazed frustration. "He played DEFENSIVE LINE," he said slowly, as if speaking to a child.

"I don't think so." Otis was either quite adamant or just pushing Smitty's buttons.

"You stupid son of a—," but before he could finish his reprimand, the chimes of the door sounded and Coach Mac and Johnny Gordon walked into the shop.

Smitty stepped away from his work and went to greet the Gordons. "Now *there's* a quarterback!" he said, smiling at Johnny.

Mac ignored the compliment. "Clean him up, Smitty."

"You got it, Coach," said Smitty, as he motioned to Johnny to sit in one of the vacant chairs. He walked back to a young man he was working on and took a few final snips before whipping off the haircutting cape and snapping it in the air to get the loose hairs off of it.

The young man stood from the barber chair and smiled as he handed Smitty money for the cut and a tip, and, as the other patron walked out, Smitty walked over to Johnny, who was nervously spinning in the chair.

"Word on the street is you had a run-in with the Melonheads last night."

Johnny turned his head and gave Smitty a curious look, but it was Mac who spoke up. "Smitty, what the hell are you talking about?"

Smitty wrapped the cape around Johnny, his eyes never leaving the coach. "C'mon Coach. You must have heard about the Melonheads." He knew as much about Melonheads as he did about football. Johnny was captivated, listening to every word Smitty was saying.

Mac wouldn't have it. "The only Melonheads I've ever seen are the ones sitting in here." His gaze shifted from Smitty to Otis and then back to Smitty.

"Oh, c'mon coach. You don't have to be mean about it. I tell you what, boy." His expression became grim. "You won't catch me driving down Wisner Road at night." He shook his head. "That's why nobody EVER drives down that way."

"Hell, NO," Otis chimed in. "You better have some candy or some shit to put on that bridge if you wanna make it out of there." Mac and Johnny looked at each other, not understanding what the hell Otis was talking about, as usual.

"They're retards, Coach," Smitty said flatly.

"You mean mentally handicapped, don't you?" said Mac, obviously offended by the remark.

"No," said Smitty, with a firmness in his voice Mac hadn't heard before. "They're retards. They sure ain't handicapped." He began trimming Johnny's hair, not missing a beat in his diatribe. "Crazy ass retards. Old

Doc Crowe was working on them when I was a boy. He turned them into crazy ass, savage, super-retards."

At this point, Johnny couldn't decide whether to think THEY were mentally handicapped or he should take them seriously.

Otis wasted no time in confirming Smitty's remarks. "That's right! Crazy ass, super-retards." He glanced at Coach Mac. "Beefcake retards."

Mac was becoming agitated. "Guys. Ease up on the retard talk. Some people get upset by that word."

"What? Retard?" Smitty was old school, raised in a time when words weren't considered offensive. "No, that don't bother nobody." He turned and addressed the people who were in his shop. "Anybody in here mad at me for saying 'retard'?"

An older man sitting in a corner chair looking through a magazine barely looked up. "Hell, no!" he said from his spot. "My brother was a retard." After a quick pause for reflection, he added, "But he wasn't no SUPER retard." The small group of old-timers sitting next to him all nodded in agreement, some adding in a 'nope' or two.

Smitty turned to the coach. "See, Coach? Nobody cares."

It was obvious that Mac DID care. He looked about the room for SOME support, but found none, even from his son, who sat there absorbing the conversation.

As he looked out the window of the shop, he noticed the office of the NEW Doc Reilly, which seemed to distract him.

He looked at Smitty and said, "Just give him a cut. I'll be back in fifteen." With that, Mac walked toward the door but, but was cut off by Otis.

"Hey, Coach," said Otis, standing a little too close. "Who's the best quarterback you ever saw?"

"Mean Joe Green, who else?" and then walked out of the shop.

Otis grinned and turned to Smitty. "See?" he said triumphantly. "I told you!"

Mac winked at Smitty, knowing full well that once Otis had a little ammunition in an argument, he wouldn't let it go. Smitty sighed, and then turned his attention back to Johnny. "Look at your hair, boy. You ain't on the hippy lettuce, are you?"

"Is he puffing the Chiba?" Otis asked, eying Johnny suspiciously.

"Ah!" piped in the old man from behind his magazine. "The chronic." Smitty and Otis looked at him in disbelief, and he quickly added, "You know. For my glaucoma."

As the men chatted, Johnny thought, *Melonheads, eh?*

CHAPTER THIRTEEN

There was a bit of a skip in his step as Mac crossed the street and walked into Doctor Reilly's office. He had been in there three times in the past—more times than he cared to—during his life in Kirtland, but he was never giddy.

There was no one at the reception desk, so Mac rang the bell. From one of the back rooms, Susan's familiar voice replied, "I'll be right there."

She has such a soothing voice, he thought as he sat in one of the chairs, snatching up a copy of 'Martha Stewart Living'. As he thumbed through it, a lemon meringue cookie recipe caught his eye.

Now THIS sounds delicious! Mac thought to himself as he carefully tore the recipe out from the magazine. Still assuming he was alone, he did not notice Susan had quietly walked into the waiting area and stood silently in the doorway for a moment watching him.

After giving him a few seconds, she spoke up. "Coach!" she said in mock anger. "Why are you mutilating my magazine?" She gave him a sideways glare as he fumbled with the magazine, clumsily putting it down, forgetting that the recipe he had just torn out was still in his hand.

"Oh, sorry," he stammered like a schoolboy caught doing something wrong by his teacher. "I cook a lot for my son and I..." he tried composing himself. "And he likes lemon flavored shit... er... STUFF, I mean."

I'm such a dick, he thought. "Sorry."

"Oh, you have a son?" Susan asked

"Yeah," replied Mac. "I just dropped him off at the barbershop. I thought I'd pop in and apologize for how some of the boys were acting yesterday." *I was acting stupid, too*, he thought, but he wasn't going to tell HER that! "I tried to warn you!"

"Like I said, no problem here." Susan smiled as she remembered. "Maybe instead you should apologize to that boy with the boner for embarrassing him!"

I can't believe she just said 'boner'! thought Mac, but said, "I was setting an example with Timmy." He was sticking with his story.

"Yeah, but how can you blame him? After all, I'm hot, right?"

Okay, she wants to play, he thought. "Did you just say 'boner'?" He puffed out his chest, challenging her.

"Yeah," she countered. "It's a medical term." She noticed that Mac was becoming a little nervous, apparently not expecting witty barbs from a woman, much less a woman *doctor*. She backed off slightly. "I'm sure I wasn't what they expected."

Mac *was* a little uncomfortable. He hadn't had an extended conversation like this with a woman since Eva left.

"No, not at all." Mac replied, smiling. "Listen, I'll get outta your hair." Hair, he thought, and remembered Johnny across the street at Smitty's. "I'm sure your busy." He turned to leave, but hesitated, and then turned back to Susan. "Doc," he said, a little surprised at himself. "Since you're new to the area, I was thinking th—"

Before he could finish his sentence, Chief Dooley suddenly popped through the door of the clinic.

"Oh, hey, Mac," he said, looking at the coach. His cop instinct picked up on the nervous tension brewing, but he chose to ignore it. There was something more important than Mac's 'carnal' urges.

"Doc," the Chief continued. "There's been an accident on Wisner Road. I need you to come down there with me." The look on his face was stern.

Susan reached behind the counter and grabbed a formidable-looking bag as she spoke. "How bad are the injuries?" she asked.

"Well, I'd say pretty bad. Like, *dead* kinda bad."

Mac cocked his head. "If he's dead, you need a coroner, not a physician."

"You got a small town here, Coach," said Dooley. "The local doctor *is* the coroner."

"I'll get my *other* bag." Susan said as she hurried off to the back room.

Dooley nodded to her as she disappeared into the back of the office. Dooley returned his attention to Mac. "I gotta come talk to your son later."

"Why?"

Dooley was quick to reply. "'Cuz he was one of the last people to see him alive."

Mac didn't understand. "Who is it?" he had started to ask, but Dooley just shook his head as Susan returned with her supplies.

Chief Dooley wasted no time heading toward the door, with full expectation that the doctor would drop whatever plans she had and simply head out with him. This was evidenced by the fact that he held the door open for her, waiting.

Susan turned to Mac before she walked out and said, "What were you about to ask me, Coach?"

A little embarrassed, he waved his hand and said, "Oh, it can wait." *Damn!*

***

Even from a distance, it was clear that anyone near the scene of the accident could see Stan's truck and propane containers strewn all over the roadway. As the police cruiser carrying Chief Dooley and Doctor Reilly approached the site, Susan was surprised to see so many emergency service personnel in the area. The area had been taped off with yellow crime scene tape that was reminiscent of crime dramas she caught herself watching from time to time on TV.

One of the deputies came over and moved the tape out of the way so the Chief and the doctor could pull into the area. "The body's over here," he said to Susan, pointing toward the front of the truck. She walked around to where he was pointing. Upon seeing Tony's mangled body, she stifled a gasp.

"Well, Chief. He's dead alright."

Dooley didn't seem amused. "Good work. So glad you came along." He became serious. "Look, I want you to help me figure out the circumstances here. If you think this was an accident or a..." He paused.

"What else could it be?" she asked. "He's lying in front of a bloodstained truck."

Dooley was unwavering. "I guess we'll know after you perform the autopsy."

"Autopsy, huh?" Susan said, stepping closer to what was left of Tony. "It's been a while."

"I'm sure it's like riding a bike, Dooley countered, as he heard himself being summoned over the radio.

"Chief Dooley, come in."

"Go ahead."

"We got a make on the driver. It's Stan McClendon."

Dooley sighed at the information. "Ol' Stan. He's a pretty straight guy. I'm surprised he didn't call this in."

"He's probably still in the woods puking," said Susan, as she hovered over Tony.

"Send a car out to his house," Dooley told the officer on the other end of the radio.

"Yes, sir." As Dooley signed off, he noticed a car coming. He recognized Mac's truck as he pulled off to the side of the road and parked. *What the hell?,* thought Dooley, as he stormed over to the vehicle just as Mac was getting out.

"Johnny," he said, looking at his son as he closed the door. "Stay in the car."

"Mac," Dooley whispered hoarsely. "What the hell are you doing here?!" He glanced toward Mac's truck and saw Johnny in the passenger seat. "I said I wanted to talk to your son, not that I wanted you to bring him here." He leaned in close to Mac. "You think he really wants to see this?" pointing to the scene. "That's Tony Scicolone down there."

Mac was visibly distraught, and Johnny immediately noticed the change in his father's face. He opened the door and got out of the truck, pushing past several of the emergency personnel.

"Dad. What's going on?"

Mac stepped in front of Johnny, not allowing him to get any closer. "It's Tony."

"What did he do?" he asked, not understanding completely what was going on.

Mac took a deep breath. "He's..." He looked at Dooley and then back at Johnny. "He's dead."

Johnny's eyes widened in disbelief. He tried to get to the front of the truck, but Dooley blocked him.

"I can't let you over there, son."

Johnny staggered back, angry and frustrated, as well as visibly shaken. He looked around the area, debating if he should push past Chief Dooley. The whole scene was chaotic, almost surreal. Johnny saw skid marks, scattered propane tanks, people in uniform bustling around, Doc Reilly hovering over something in front of the truck...

... but he didn't see the large mutant creature with the hose gushing fluids—the MELONHEAD - hiding in the brush. Watching. The thing sees a familiar face.

Johnny.

Johnny looked at Dooley, who was still blocking his way. "Did those things get him?" Dooley looked at him strangely. "From last night. Those freaks!"

Dooley shook his head. "No, those things didn't get him. He was hit by a truck."

Mac stepped up to them. "Didn't you take him home last night?"

Johnny looked like a deer caught in headlights. He looked back and forth from Mac to Chief Dooley, not knowing what to say. The silence was deafening, as everyone, including Susan turned and looked at him. He tried to figure out the best course of action. The words his father had told him, '*truth always wins out*', echoed in his head. He straightened up and looked at all of the adults around him, focusing finally on his father.

"No," he said flatly. "He asked me to pull over and drop him off out here."

Mac was stunned, as was everyone else who was within earshot. "At four in the morning?!" He lowered his voice, trying to remain calm. "You dropped him off here?!"

"Not here," Johnny replied. "More like a quarter mile up the road."

"Are you shittin' me?!" Dooley said, almost shouting.

Mac shook his head in disbelief. "Why?!" Off in the distance, Susan watched as the two men interrogated Johnny. She saw how difficult it was for him to answer their questions. She admired his courage in the face of such tragedy.

"Well," he began. "I knew we had to go to the police, but Tony had this big bag of weed, so I threw it out the window, and..."

"Johnny," Mac said. "Weed?!"

Johnny had been lectured about the evils of cannabis, and he appreciated his father's concern, which is why he never partook of it. "Not me, dad," he assured Mac. "I swear. That was Tony's thing. He wanted to look for it."

"Thanks, Johnny," said Dooley. "That's all I need." He looked around the scene. "Stoned kid, wasted out of his mind, staggers out of the woods in front of a semi."

Johnny was quick to defend his friend. "He wouldn't have stuck around to get stoned."

"Well," Dooley countered. "He was brave enough to wander around by himself for weed, Champ."

Johnny was growing frantic. "It was those things, those freaks. The Melonheads!"

Dooley was reaching his wits end. "What the fuck are you talking about?"

Almost embarrassed, Mac jumped in. "Johnny!"

Johnny wouldn't be stopped. "The Melonheads!" He looked from Mac to Dooley. "Old Doc Crowe was experimenting on kids with water on the brain back in the fifties and they're still alive. Living in the woods." He paused, and then added, "And they, they like candy."

Dooley roared with laughter despite being in the middle of such a macabre scene. "Candy!" he muttered.

Mac tried to explain. "Sorry, Chief. The old timers at Smitty's put that into his head." He glared at Johnny.

Dooley rubbed his face. "Oh, those idiots." He put his hand on Mac's shoulder. "Mac, just take him home. I'd like to find old Stan before the sun goes down." He paused and then said, "And all this fairy tale bullshit is just pissing me off." He turned to Johnny, and with a snide look and a sarcastic tone, said, "See ya', Champ." Almost as an insulting afterthought, he added, "Like your haircut." He turned to walk away.

"He's right," said Susan.

Dooley stopped and turned. "Excuse me?"

Susan looked at Johnny. "Johnny? That's your name?" Johnny nodded. "Well, you're right. He was running."

Dooley grew intense. "What makes you say that, Dr. Reilly?" He had a tone of bitter sarcasm in his voice.

Without missing a beat DOCTOR Reilly responded. "He's got scratches on his arms." She pointed to Tony's body. "Mild abrasions all over him, like he was..." she thought for a second, "...running fast, not stopping. Running from something."

"Could it have been," his voice dripping with condescending sarcasm, "a big truck?" he asked, pointing to the vehicle.

As Doctor Reilly shook her head at the obviously ignorant response from Chief Dooley, Mac grabbed Johnny by the arm and pulled him off to the side, near his truck. Neither one of them noticed the fluid-gushing Melonhead glaring at Johnny from the shadows, vengeance in his wild eyes.

As the mutant watched from a distance, Mac tried to remain calm in the face of calamity. "Until I figure out what to do with you, I want you to stay at the house."

Johnny was shocked, and a little insulted. "Are you grounding me?" he asked, and then boldly challenged, "I'm eighteen."

Mac would not hear it. "And still under my roof, so, yes, I'm grounding you." He grabbed onto Johnny's arm and pulled him to within inches of his face. "You're acting nuts, and what you do is a reflection on me."

"Sorry about tarnishing your reputation, Dad." He shook his arm from Mac's grasp. "Mom would have believed me."

Johnny had crossed the line. "Mom!" he huffed. "Don't you even MENTION her. She left us and she never looked back."

Johnny became defensive. "She didn't leave US," he said angrily. "She left YOU."

Mac was slightly taken aback by his son's sudden boldness. "You're definitely grounded. Tell Ziggy you're in lockdown." Johnny stomped his foot, much like an angry child, and was about to argue with his father, but was interrupted by Susan calling to Mac from the front of the truck.

"Hey, Mac? Think you could give me a ride back?"

Mac looked at Johnny, almost waiting for him to supply a smug response. "Yeah. Gimme a minute," he replied.

The fluid-gushing Melonhead's attention was drawn to Susan. There was something oddly familiar about her. The creature watched as Susan reached into her pocket and pulled out a butterscotch hard candy, unwrapped it, and popped it into her mouth.

He watched. And remembered.

CHAPTER FOURTEEN
Flashback, 1964

The young boy heard the footsteps of someone coming down the stairs and turned his deformed head to see who it was. Was it his tormentor, coming back to hurt him some more? He glanced over at his brother and sister, still unconscious, and strapped to a table just like he was. He turned his head back to see Dr. Crowe's feet appear, and then the rest of his body. But what's this? There was another person behind him. He craned his neck to try and get a better look, since his eyes were farther apart than 'normal' people. He was just a child, but there was more to him, physical deformities notwithstanding.

A lovely woman followed the evil man. She had gentle eyes and a soft footfall, unlike the cold glare and hurried clatter the doctor had. He moaned as they approached. The woman hesitated, but the doctor held out his hand, beckoning her closer. "It's alright, Marilyn. They can't hurt you," he said, as she slowly moved closer to the child's gurney.

This was the first time she had been downstairs in quite some time, and as she looked around the room, she was startled that it had been transformed into a full-blown laboratory. She scanned the room, seeing strange equipment, but, what disturbed her most was the presence of seven hospital-type beds, each one occupied by a hydrocephalic child, their deformed heads lolling back and forth in a sedated stupor. There were four boys and three girls and she guessed at the ages being somewhere between seven and fourteen. The largest one, a boy with a very large head, larger than the rest, watched her come near, his head constantly shifting left and right. "Come closer, darling," said Crowe, holding out his hand.

As Marilyn stepped closer, she noticed the straps holding the boy down. "Why the restraints?" she asked as she stood next to her husband.

"Just so they don't injure themselves," he quickly replied. The boy on the bed pulled at his bonds as if he understood what they were talking about. Marilyn looked at the boy.

"Are they dangerous?"

"No. They're quite docile." Then he added, "Unfortunately, with this condition, their life expectancy isn't very long. They're orphans. Abandoned." He walked around, pausing at each one of the beds as he continued. "They need someone to take care of them." He looked directly into Marilyn's eyes. There was something very convincing in his tone.

He smiled at her, and he realized by the look on her face, the way she looked at the 'children', that a 'motherly' instinct had taken over, just as he had hoped. The large deformed youngster on the bed noticed it as well. He sensed that this was a kind and gentle woman, unlike the man. He looked up at her.

"Hello," he said, surprising Marilyn. She turned to her husband.

"He can talk!" she said

"Sure he can," replied Crowe, his smile never faltering. "He's a person after all."

Marilyn stepped closer to the bed, leaning in just a little bit. "Hello," she said smiling. As she moved closer, she reached into her sweater pocket and pulled out something light-brown in color, wrapped in plastic. She always kept a supply of butterscotch hard candy in her pocket. *My addiction*, she would often say.

"Do you want some candy?" she asked the boy.

As an afterthought, she turned to Crowe and said, "Can he have..." the Doctor nodded, and she continued unwrapping the candy. She looked into the child's face and smiled, and the boy's eyes widened in anticipation.

"Yes, candy!" he said, and followed it with a typical child-like, "Mmmmm!" As she finished unwrapping the candy, she steeped closer and carefully dropped it into his open, waiting mouth. As the young deformed boy savored the flavor of the butterscotch, his parakeet-like eyes rolled in delight. "Good," he purred, the candy crunching in is misshapen teeth.

As the boy enjoyed the treat, the other children began to emerge from their sedated state, and turned to watch their 'brother' partaking in something good. Marilyn saw them stirring, as they started moaning. Not in fear or pain, but in a sort of childlike request for butterscotch candy. She smiled as she looked around the room at each one of them. The doctor also smiled.

"I hope you have enough for everyone," he said as he watched her heart melt.

"I'll run upstairs and get some more," she said excitedly, walking quickly, almost dashing, to the stairs to get more 'treats' for the children.

The doctor's eyes followed her as she disappeared up the stairs, and then he turned and looked at the large child, watching as he crunched at the last bit of the candy. His demeanor was almost sadistic. "Enjoy this moment," he whispered, "for tonight your *treatment* begins."

CHAPTER FIFTEEN

Mac stepped into his truck. Susan got in on the passenger side and Johnny pushing himself in after her. As Mac started off down the road, she offered each of them a piece of candy, both of them smiling but declining her offer. *More for me,* she thought, as she popped another into her mouth. She looked over at Johnny, who was staring out the window, apparently lost in thought.

"Hydrocephalus," she said to Johnny, who looked back at her, confused. "That's the disease, by the way." He still seemed confused. "The 'water on the brain' you were talking about?"

"Yeah! That's it," he replied, finally understanding what she was referring to. "That's what Otis said. Hydrocephalus."

Susan nodded. "I wouldn't worry though. Children with that disease rarely lived past their mid-teens back then." She thought for a moment, remembering that Johnny had mentioned Doctor Crowe, who had practiced at that time. "The fifties, early sixties?" she queried. "They'd be long dead by now." She tried to sound reassuring.

Johnny was quick to respond. "No," he said. "He pumped 'em full of chemicals and stuff. Government crap like agent orange." He turned and looked at Mac, who rolled his eyes as Johnny spoke. "He turned them into animals."

Mac had enough of Johnny's nonsense. "Alright, seriously!" he said, frustrated, as he turned the vehicle into the Gordon driveway. "I'm done! Otis?! You believe Otis?!"

"Ask any old timer," Johnny said defensively. "They'll tell you." Johnny then added, "And, no, Dad. I believe my own EYES. I saw them, and I think..." he paused, an uncomfortable expression crossing his face, "these things are trying to get me. Like revenge for hitting their brother." He thought for a second. "Or nephew, or whatever!"

Mac glanced over Susan to Johnny. "Well, then it's a good thing you'll be locked in the house." He put the truck in PARK. "Go!" Johnny shook his head and huffed as he jumped out of the truck and went inside. He watched as Johnny unlocked the front door and went inside, and then looked over at Susan, who was looking at him and smiling.

She slowly slid out from the center of the bench seat into the passenger side. They looked at each other, as Mac backed out of the driveway and headed toward Main Street to Susan's office. "New York, huh?" Mac said as they drove, trying for light, 'neutral' conversation. "Why'd you leave?"

Susan looked out the window as she pondered the answer. "Big city, bright lights. That never impressed me. I like it calm. Those big ER's you see so much..." she thought, searching for the right word, "...pain. So many injuries." Her eyes closed as she remembered. "And you think, *how can people act like such animals?* Like what happened to your son's friend."

She grew frustrated. "All the time. It gets to be too much."

She finished her thought as they pulled into the parking lot by her office. "Has Johnny ever lied to you before?" she inquired, hoping she hadn't crossed any lines by asking.

Mac didn't seem to mind. "Sure, little things."

Susan pressed on. "But something like this? The Melonheads?"

Mac turned and looked at her. "No," he replied. "Why?"

Susan shrugged as she climbed out of Mac's truck. She turned and smiled.

"Come by later," she said and closed the door. Mac watched her go inside to wait for Tony's body to be brought in.

***

Mac stood in the corner of the room as Susan began examining Tony's body. Despite the fact that he had been struck full-on by a truck and much of the remains resembled raspberry pulp, Susan did her best examining what was there, hoping to get answers. Mac almost envied her, not in the job that she was doing, but that she hadn't vomited. HE, on the other hand, was feeling a bit 'green'. She leaned in a little closer before reaching for a magnifying glass. "This kid must have been running his butt off," she said. "Something spooked him."

"What do you mean?" Mac asked, not looking in her direction.

"Well, these abrasions," pointing to the scratches on what was left of Tony's face and arms. "They're not very deep, but there's just so many of them." She straightened herself and stretched, her back cracking audibly.

"So, he ran through a bush." Mac concluded.

"If you scratch yourself, you slow down so it doesn't happen again," Susan continued. "And some of these are on the *back* of his arms." Susan lifted her arms, showing Mac what position Tony's arms were probably in as he ran.

A look of understanding crossed Mac's face. "He saw the bushes."

"Yeah," said Susan, "and ran through them." She turned to her instrument table and picked up a scalpel and brought it over Tony's stomach.

Mac stepped back. "What are you doing?" he asked, perhaps a little too quickly. He wasn't exactly squeamish, but he didn't want the doctor - no, SUSAN - to think he was a wuss. Considering the situation, Susan smiled.

"Well, I'll be." She turned and looked at Mac. "Big tough coach is squeamish?"

She must be reading my mind, he thought. "This is my first autopsy."

"There's a bucket over there if you get sick." Mac cleared his throat and walked over to the pail Susan had pointed to, picked it up and held it to his chest.

"You're a terrible flirter," he said.

Susan's eyes widened in mock surprise. "Is that what I'm doing?" She paused and looked at Mac pensively. "Actually, is there a reason why you're here, Coach? You don't have to stay."

Mac tried his best to hide a look of disappointment, and puffed up a little, bravado prevailing. "I just wanted to make sure you were alright." As he shuffled nervously, Susan saw something around Mac's neck catch the light. It was a little gold key on a chain. She decided to change the topic.

"What's your story with that necklace? The big Coach with such a dainty key."

Mac's hand went to the key. "Oh," he said as he rubbed it between his fingers. "My wife gave that to me. It's the key to her heart." He paused for a moment. "Ex-wife, kinda," he said, trying to correct himself.

Susan didn't miss a beat. "Ex-wife kinda? How's that work?"

"She left me. Us." he quickly added. "Me and my son. We got in a fight. We'd been fighting." Mac turned slightly, reliving the memory. "She just packed a bag and called a cab. Never heard from her after that."

Susan was curious. "Why wear it then?"

Mac shrugged. "I don't know. I guess I just never..." he paused, uncomfortable with the direction of the conversation, "...took it off." *That's it*, he thought, and shifted the topic. "You cutting me up or the boy?" A few seconds of awkward silence followed, as Susan turned back to work on Tony's body

"Okay," she said, lifting the scalpel. "Here we go." She carefully lowered the scalpel, touching the pale flesh of Tony's stomach. From her peripheral vision, she noticed Mac grip the bucket tighter, when the bell from the reception area sounded. Mac let out an audible sigh.

"Saved by the bell," Susan said, as she put the scalpel down carefully and walked to the front. As she got closer to the reception area, she heard the familiar rhythmic tapping of fingers on the counter, followed by a loud crunching sound. She knew who it was before she reached the front and smiled.

"Three minutes to come to reception?" Doc Reilly - OLD Doc Reilly - asked in mock anger. "What if I was bleeding out my eyes?"

"Are you bleeding out your eyes, Grandpa?"

"Not this time. But you never know," he replied smiling, as he met Susan half way around the reception desk and gave her a big hug. He stepped back and put his hands around her face as if she was a little girl, and kissed her forehead. "How's my little girl?"

"Good," Susan replied. "Busy. About to start an autopsy."

Old Doc Reilly's expression became serious. "I heard," he said. "Thought I'd come and—"

"Help?" Susan quickly interjected. "Great!"

"See how you're doing." he corrected "But I guess I COULD help."

He looked at Susan. "Why?" he asked. "Been a while?" Just as he was speaking, Coach Mac walked into the reception area.

"You just gonna leave me in there?" he asked, and then saw the senior Reilly standing next to Susan.

"Oh! Hey, Doc," Mac said, as he walked over to Doc Reilly and shook his hand. "We missed you at practice this year." He gestured toward Susan. "I wish I'd known."

"Ah, yes!" Reilly said. "How are my big boys doing? Who'd you get to come out for the turn and cough this year?" He smiled. "Doc Amidon?"

Mac shook his head. "No. Not Doc Amidon." He turned and looked over at Susan. Realization dawned on the elder Reilly and he burst out laughing.

"Noooo!" he chortled as he tried to regain some *professional* composure. "That must have been a sight." He wiped tears from his eyes. "I wish I had been there. Those poor boys."

"Poor boys?" Susan shot back. "It wasn't a joyride for me, ya' know."

Still chuckling lightly, Reilly said, "Of THAT I'm sure, my dear." He moved close to her and put an arm around her shoulder. "Of that, I'm sure."

Mac realized he was still holding onto the pail. As he put it down he said, "Speaking of which, I have to get to practice."

"Chicken," Susan said, flashing him a big grin.

As Mac was walking out, he stopped and turned back to her. "Are you doing anything tonight?" he asked.

"No," she replied. "No plans."

Seizing the opportunity while his courage held, he said, "Well, one of the teachers has this annual tiki party. Big bash." He glanced at the senior Doc Reilly, almost looking for approval, and then looked back at her. "After a day like today, I thought maybe you'd wanna get out a little bit." He shyly looked down and then, realizing that he was acting like one of his freshman students, then looked back up. "Meet some people. I mean, if you'll be done here."

Susan's eyes lit up. "Yeah, sure," she replied. "That would be great."

"This guy makes the best kielbasa burgers," Mac said, trying to 'sell' the event.

"Kielbasa burgers," Susan said, nodding. "Awesome!"

Almost as an afterthought, Mac turned to Doc Reilly. "Doc, you're invited too, of course."

"Thank you, Coach," said Reilly with a smirk. "I already have my invitation."

Mac turned his attention back to Susan and said, "Pick you up at eight?"

Susan nodded once and smiled. "I'll be here."

She has SUCH a nice smile, Mac thought as he walked out of the office.

Doc Reilly couldn't miss the opportunity to chide his granddaughter.

"My little girl has a crush on the coach, I see," he said with a wink.

"What?" said Susan, almost insulted. "Don't be silly."

"I know you do."

Susan took a defiant stance. "How's that?"

"Kielbasi burger, eh?" He gave her sideways glance. "Aren't you still a vegetarian?"

Busted! All Susan could say was, "Ah!"

***

There was a noticeable spring in Mac's step as he walked out of Doc Reilly's - BOTH Doc Reillys, in fact - office and strolled down Main Street. huge smile was plastered across his face. Jesse Putnam, or 'Sparky' as everyone called him, was doing his daily rounds of delivering the mail.

"Hello, Sparky," Mac bellowed. "Big date tonight!" As he walked past the obviously confused Sparky, Mac saw Mary on the other side of the street and waved to her.

"Hey, Mary," Mac called. "I got a BIG date tonight!"

"BIG date?" she said with a smile, mocking Mac's enthusiasm.

"That's right, baby!" he replied as he continued bopping down the street.

***

As Susan turned and headed back to continue the autopsy, her grandfather scanned the reception desk, a panicked expression crossing his face. "Where's the candy?" he called behind her. "Susan!" He was serious. "Where's my bowl of candy?!"

Susan turned. "What are you talking about?"

"My butterscotches. My bowl of hard candy." He tapped loudly on the table. "There's supposed to be a bowl of hard candy on this counter all the time!" For emphasis he added, "For customers!" He put his hands on his hips as if scolding a child. "Everybody knows when you visit Doc Reilly's office, there's butterscotchies. It's been here for over forty years and…" but before he could finish his sentence, Susan reached under the reception desk and pulled out a candy dish, brimming with butterscotch hard candies.

"I just moved 'em when I was wiping the counter earlier." She waved her hand over the dish like a magician. "See? Don't give yourself a heart attack."

Old Doc Reilly sighed. "I know this is YOUR practice now, but it's the one thing I want you to keep the same." He looked down, almost pouting. "I know it's little—"

"No, I know." Susan understood what he was saying. "That's like your trademark? Always giving out candy?" As she said this, she picked up one of the candies and pitched it to her grandfather and then got one for herself. As she unwrapped her candy, she said, "Don't worry. The bowl stays. I love these things just as much as you do." She popped it into her mouth. "You're the jerk that got me hooked on 'em," she said in a scolding voice. "I always have a pocketful." As she headed to the back room, she stopped and turned. "Hey, Gramps?" she said with a questioning tone. "Tell me about Doctor Crowe."

The older Doc Reilly's expression tightened and grew serious, all remnants of jocularity dissipating at the mention of that name. He sighed. "Crowe?"

CHAPTER SIXTEEN

Mac stood at the sidelines watching the team practice - the offense was running plays while the defense was running tackling drills. Mac was in full 'Coach Gordon' mode, his mind running plays and practically foretelling what each man on his team was going to do in any particular situation. He taught them well, how to play fair and to keep their lives outside the team fair as well. He watched as Craig and Ron walked over to the water hose to get a drink at the same time that Joe waddled over to fill some empty bottles. Joe was a bit 'slow', but he loved his job. Mac referred to him as a 'coach', and requested that his team do the same. With one eye on the plays being run, the other watched what was happening by the water hose.

"Hey, guys," Joe said, addressing Ron and Craig. "Mind if I use the hose? I need to fill these bottles."

Craig looked at Ron and winked. "Sure, Joe," he said. "You need some water?" He pretended to hand Joe the hose, but squirted him in the face instead. "Here's your water!" he spewed, venom in his voice, as Joe sputtered and spit out the water.

Suddenly, Craig kicked the basket of empty bottles out of Joe's hands. "Stupid retard!" he shouted.

Mac stormed toward them.

***

From a hidden spot in the woods, Peter Walls was watching the team practice. He wanted to get some dirt on the team, especially Coach Mac, since he had the nerve to ban him from coming to any practice sessions. He crouched out of sight of the coach and the team, camera ready. *All right*, he thought, as he watched the activity between Joe and the two team members. *Some action!*

When Coach Mac stalked over to them, he began snapping photos. "Uh-oh!" he said aloud. "You boys are in trouble!"

Suddenly something, a person perhaps, flashed behind Peter and shuffled in the woods. Peter quickly turned toward the noise but saw nothing.

"Damn squirrels," he said, and turned back to the activity on the field.

***

Mac quickened his pace toward Joe, as Craig began kicking the empty water bottles out of his reach, not allowing him to pick them up. Craig had handed the hose to Ron, who continued to spray Joe. "What's the matter, dummy," Craig said mockingly. "Can't get your bottles?"

Ron didn't notice Coach Gordon looming up behind him until Mac's foot came up and kick Ron in the butt. Ron wheeled around in surprise, squirting the coach in his pants.

Mac became furious and grabbed Ron by the face mask, yanking the hose from his hand and pushing him to the ground, spraying him directly in the face, and then slapped him in the helmet.

From his hidden position in the woods, Peter Walls watched and snapped pictures of the incident. "You can't kick the kids, Coach," he muttered with glee.

Also watching from the woods was the fluid-gushing Melonhead, who was standing just a few feet from Walls. He watched as the coach kicked Ron in the butt. He watched as the coach grabbed Ron by the face mask. He watched as the coach slapped Ron in the helmet.

He watched.

And remembered.

***

From his gurney, the large young Melonhead watched as Doctor Crowe stood above one of his smaller 'siblings' and slapped him repeatedly in the head. "Shut up!" Crowe shouted as he slapped the smaller Melonhead again and again, who, at this point, was crying uncontrollably. "Shut up! I'm SICK of the constant noise!" As Crowe raised his hand higher for what would have been a very hard damaging blow, the large, young Melonhead raised himself as high as he could against his restraints.

"Stop!" cried the large Melonhead, as Crowe turned and glared at the source of the challenge.

"Who are you to tell me to stop?" Crowe growled as he slowly walked to the boy helplessly strapped to the table, his anger escalating with each step closer. "You don't EVER tell me what to do," he screamed as he brought his hand crashing down onto his 'patient'.

***

The large Melonhead snapped back to the present and watched as Coach Mac turned his anger from Ron to Craig, grabbing him by the face mask.

"What the fuck do you think you're doing?" he shouted into Craig's face. "You think this is funny?"

From his submissive position, Craig practically whimpered, "C'mon, Coach. We're just playing with him."

"Playing with him!" Mac was fuming. "He's a forty-four-year-old man! He's not to be *played* with." Mac pulled Craig's face closer to his. "I've known that man since I was five years old, and I'm NOT gonna let you two assholes screw with him," and pushed Craig into the ground. "I want the two of you off this team."

From a distance, Coach Morelli saw Mac yelling at Craig and Ron and rushed over to them.

Craig stood up. "My dad isn't gonna be happy about this," he said, almost threatening.

"Too bad," Mac countered, not giving in to Craig's 'challenge', as the two bullies skulked away

Craig turned, continuing to walk backwards away from Mac. "Good luck repeating without two of your starters."

"You little punk," Mac said as he was about to charge at Craig before being intercepted by Coach

Morelli. Morelli quickly stepped between the boys and the angry Mac.

"Mac, calm down," he said, holding up his hands. "Let them go. You don't need the headache."

From his secret perch in the woods, Peter Walls continued snapping pictures, smoking a cigarette as he did. "Thanks, Coach," he chuckled. "You just gave me the biggest story of the year." He took one last long draw of his cigarette and flicked it away without looking where he pitched it, which, unfortunately for Peter, was right at the fluid-gushing Melonhead.

Peter continued snapping photos as the cigarette bounced off the Melonhead's chest and onto the ground. "Too bad, Coach. Looks like you were about to have another undefeated—" but his musing was interrupted by the giant Melonhead, who grabbed the strap of Peter Walls' camera and yanked it tight, pulling the camera to his throat and crushing his windpipe.

As Walls struggled to get free, he felt a sudden massive pain in the center of his back, just as the Melonhead's fist came crashing through his ribcage and out of his chest, clenching his still-beating heart, which was the last thing Peter Walls saw as his head slumped down and hit his camera, which snapped a photo of that heart.

CHAPTER SEVENTEEN

"The man was crazy!" Old Doc Reilly said to Susan as they were performing the autopsy on Tony. "He dealt in fantasy, not science." As he spoke, Susan watched him examining the body, both fascinated and impressed at his proficiency, even at his age.

"Tell me about the kids he worked with," she said, looking up at him.

He glanced at Susan with a questioning look. "Have you been hearing strange stories about the Melonheads?"

He must be able to read my mind, she thought. "I've heard a few."

"To his credit," Reilly began, "the man was one fine neurologist. But, he kept fooling with those poor kids."

"Fooling?" Susan was captivated.

"Insisting he could cure them. Trying experimental procedures." He stood up straight, pointing to the equipment in the room. "We didn't have the technology back then to fix them."

"What happened with the doctor?" she asked.

Her grandfather seemed reluctant to continue, and Susan began to think he was trying to hide something. After a pause, the old man sighed. He knew she could be tenacious when she wanted something.

"He became obsessed with those children," he continued. "Some of them went missing from the clinic." Another pause and a breath. "That's how I knew him. The clinic. He told me some had died, some were transferred." He shook his head and looked back at Tony as he continued his story. "I was never able to find any paperwork to verify his story. Just as I was about to report him to the Board of Regents, he and his wife were killed in a house fire."

"So you never told anyone?" she asked, sounding almost like an accusation.

The elder Reilly felt the need to explain. "The man was dead, baby. At that point, it would have been useless. All of his brilliant work beforehand tarnished because of arrogant decisions." He slammed his hands on the edge of the autopsy table, startling Susan. "Crazy, arrogant decisions! Affecting so many other people."

Susan was surprised. She had never seen her grandfather become so emotional. She didn't press him further, and they continued the autopsy in relative silence except to record their findings and theories.

CHAPTER EIGHTEEN

Several hours had passed since Tony's body was brought to Doctor Reilly —BOTH Doctor Reillys— to be autopsied, and the emergency crews had all but cleared the entire area. The inventory sheet from Stan McClendon's indicated that there were twenty containers of propane, but the search and clean-up only yielded eleven. Chief Dooley made the decision to continue the search the next day, and sent the remaining crew home. After everyone else left, he stayed on-site a bit longer, hoping to find some answers.. He preferred to work alone in certain circumstances and this was one of them.

There were questions rolling around in his mind, the first was: could this be some drug-induced story and could Otis' tale just be some kind of excuse for something more tragic? Dooley didn't think so, because, no matter how out-of-control Johnny Gordon seemed, he knew Mac Gordon, and Mac would never allow his son to start down a path of drug abuse, especially after Eva walked out on them.

Another question was where could those nine missing containers be? *Propane tanks are not exactly small*, he thought, as he scoured the woods as the light faded. He looked up and around, and stretched out his back, an audible crack reverberating through the woods. *This 'getting old' shit sucks*, he thought as he scanned the area.

"Stan! Claudio!" he called out into the waning light. "You out there?! If you can hear me, say something!" *If they could say something, they would have by now*, he thought. He was beginning to lose hope in finding either one of them. Alive, anyway. As he walked deeper into the woods, he reached into his pocket and withdrew an ornate flask—a birthday gift from his officers some years back—that was filled with a half-and-half mix of Nob Hill and Jack Daniels, opened it and took a long slow swig of the golden nectar. After a hard swallow and a good clearing of his throat, he called out again. "C'mon! If you're hurt, I can help."

He scanned the area, his eyes adjusting to the fading light, and thought he saw someone in the distance. He recapped the flask and began walking toward the person who was leaning against a tree. As he got closer, he realized that it was a woman.

"Hello," he said, making as much noise as he could so she would not think he was stalking her.

"Ma'am? This is Chief Dooley of Kirtland P.D."

He moved closer. "Ma'am, you okay?"

As he drew closer and his eyes focused, he noticed the outline—the FIGURE—of this woman. He couldn't make out her features, but her body was spectacular. *Wow!* thought Dooley. *What would someone like THIS be out here at this time of day?*

A few steps closer and he saw her silhouette, showing a pair of perfect breasts and a very tight butt. Finely-chiseled legs protruded from a pair of Daisy-Duke short-shorts.

Dooley was feeling fluttering in his loins. *Butterflies*, he mused. *But it's time to keep it real, keep it professional.* "Excuse me," he said, feeling the warmth of the bourbon mix coursing through him. "Have you seen anyone out here this evening?"

The woman, still leaning against the tree, didn't say anything, nor did she turn. She just shook her head.

Dooley decided to continue speaking. "I'm looking for a man about sixty years old. And a tall Dago." *Oh, man!* he thought. *Too much liquor. Dago? Really?!*

Still no verbal response from the voluptuous figure. Instead, she arched her back and began rubbing her hand seductively over her thigh.

Dooley could not help ogling her. Partly from being a little tired and partly (mostly) from the alcohol, he realized he was getting excited. He decided to press his luck. "You know, a pretty girl like you shouldn't be out in the woods at night all by yourself."

For the first time, she let out a sound—a long drawn-out, VERY sexy moan—as she continued rubbing her body, moving up from her thigh to her hip, closing in on her breasts..

"Say what?" said Dooley, a little startled. He was greeted with another moan, sexier than the first.

"That's the nicest thing I've heard all day," Dooley continued, in his most charming voice.

He reached out and put his hand on her shoulder.

Another moan.

Dooley grew more excited, as he boldly decided to try for second base. "What's your name, honey?" he said, as he turned her to face him…

… and froze in horror at the visage that greeted him!

One half of this woman's face was beautiful, but the other half was completely disfigured. Half of her forehead was huge and bulging, almost to the point of bursting. Her left eye was disproportionately positioned and the left side of her mouth was drooping. She was missing patches of hair, and there was a nearly non-existent ear.

"What the fuck?!" Dooley screamed as he recoiled in shock. His police instinct and training kicked in, knocking out any effects of alcohol. He quickly reached for his gun, but the siren/monstrosity was lightning fast, and grabbed his arm, preventing him from reaching his holster. As Dooley tried in vain to jerk free, she/it let out the most horrible scream Dooley had ever heard.

God DAMN, he thought. *This bitch is STRONG!* "Let me go, you bitch!" Dooley exclaimed, as the ground behind him lifted—a trap door was hidden under the brush.

Suddenly, the gymnast-looking Melonhead that had chased Tony to his death sprang up from the opening and grabbed Dooley's legs and pulled him toward the hole.

Dooley clutched onto a tree root with all his might. *This bastard is NOT going to get me*, Dooley thought, as he held on to the tree, reaching with the other hand to get a better two-handed hold. As he began to pull free from the grip of his attacker, another patch of ground opened, and the housecoat-wearing Melonhead emerged and crawled toward Dooley like a deranged giant spider.

Before Dooley could look up and see the second nemesis, the housecoat Melonhead reached out and tore Dooley's arm from the elbow joint. Dooley shrieked in pain and shock as blood sprayed from the stump that once held the rest of his arm.

With his two-hand advantage gone, the gymnast Melonhead easily yanked the still-screaming Dooley into the hole in the ground. As the earthen trap door closed around him, Dooley's screams became lost in the underground den of the Melonheads

CHAPTER NINETEEN

Tony was always the best of the three of us, thought Johnny as he sat on the couch in his living room playing video games. He couldn't believe it. Tony, Ziggy and he were the Three Amigos, The Three Stooges, The Bee Gees (a joke that someone had made about them a few years back that, unfortunately, stuck). They were going to crash the tiki party, but between Tony getting killed and him being grounded, that wasn't in the cards.

Cujo, curled up in Johnny's lap, yawned contentedly and stretched as Johnny continued to play, but paid no attention to what he was doing. They both glanced up when they heard Mac coming down the stairs. With an unusual spring in his step, the normally stoic Coach Mac Gordon came bouncing down the stairs adorned in a LOUD Hawaiian shirt, accented by a neon flower lei. He hopped down the last three steps and stopped in front of the mirror, checking his hair. As he ran his right hand over his coiffed locks, he tossed an equally gaudy Hawaiian shirt to Johnny. It landed on Cujo's head, who wisely shook it off. "Here," he said as Johnny cocked his head at the image that he wished wasn't his father. "You better get ready."

Johnny looked at him questioningly. "Ready for what?"

"Doug's tiki party," and with another glance in the mirror, Mac added, "Is my air thinning?"

"Yes," Johnny snapped back quickly, which got him a dirty look, and then said, "I wasn't invited," and with a smug look, added, "Warden."

Not missing a beat, Mac said, "You weren't INVITED. You were VOLUNTEERED."

"Volunteered for what?" Johnny asked, not liking what he knew was coming.

"You'll be serving drinks, hors d'oeuvres, dumping ashtrays. Whatever Doug needs. It's part of lock down," he said, and then, hoping to show Johnny the bright side, added, "Hey! At least it's a party."

Johnny knew he needed to get out of the house, and to get his mind off the events of the last day. "Give me a few minutes to get ready," he said as he gently put Cujo down and got off the couch.

"Can't," said Mac, a little too happily. "I have to go pick up Doc Reilly."

"Why you driving him?"

"No," replied Mac with a grin. "The OTHER one. Susan." The silence between father and son—and Cujo—was deafening, until Johnny spoke up a few seconds later.

"A date?" he asked. "What? I'm like a waiter on your date?" Johnny was a little taken aback. His father was going out—with a *woman*.

"It's not a date," Mac said, trying to justify the plan. "She's new in town." He glanced at his watch. "And I'm late."

Johnny followed Mac to the door. "How am I gonna get there?" Johnny protested. "The van is in the shop."

"It's only a couple of miles," replied Mac as he rushed down the steps and opened the door of his truck. "Take your bike."

A look of concern mixed with fear crossed Johnny's face. "No, Dad, listen," he said. "Please! I seriously think those things are—"

But before he could finish, Mac shouted, "TAKE THE BIKE!" as he drove off down the street.

CHAPTER TWENTY

The tunnel was dark and muddy as the fluid-gushing Melonhead slid down into the lair: a large chamber filled with clothes, bicycles hub caps old pieces of scrap. It was a collection chamber for the Melonheads, where they brought everything they scavenged to be 'inventoried'. The Gusher wasn't empty-handed, for he dragged Peter Walls' body into the chamber and unceremoniously dropped it like an old sack next to several propane tanks. Stepping over what could be considered 'essential supplies' in the Melonhead world, he walked out into another corridor where he heard high-pitched wailing, as if someone had amplified the sound of fingernails scraping across a blackboard.

He entered another chamber, not as large as the first, that had something that looked like cradles scooped out of the muddy walls, each one occupied by a baby Melonhead. There were eight in all, each one with a swollen head with distorted features, whether it was eyes on the sides or drooping facial features. The pressure of water on the brain, or hydrocephalia, seemed almost too much for them, as they wailed in considerable pain.

The Gusher seemed agitated, almost angered, by the noise emitting from these miniature monsters. The fluid draining from the hose in his head squirted even more as he held his hands over his ears, trying to cover the noise of the baby Melonheads. The more agitated he became, the more fluid drained from the end of the hose.

With his hands still cupped over his ears, he walked through the 'nursery' and into another room, where an older female Melonhead sat. She was haggard-looking and 'skanky', dressed in dirty, ragged clothing. She sat with her deformed breast exposed, trying to nurse a baby Melonhead. The baby, which was smaller than the ones in the previous room, cried louder than the other eight.

The Gusher stormed over to the she-beast as she tried in vain to breast-feed the screaming baby, snatched it from her arms, and twisted its head completely around, snapping its neck with a loud crack. Shrieks of what seemed to be protest came from the Skank Melonhead as she leaped from her seat and charged the Gusher, only to be halted mid-leap when his hand grabbed her by the throat.

He lifted her slightly, her feet almost dangling, but, instead of giving her the same 'fate' he gave to the baby, he just glared menacingly into her face and threw her across the room. As the Gusher stalked out of that room and headed into the next, she quickly crawled to the body of the baby Melonhead and cradled it in her arms, forcing its dead lips to her naked breast.

"Get me the fuck outta here!" the Gusher heard as he walked along another muddy corridor to yet another chamber, where Chief Dooley was lashed to a wall by the neck, and a make-shift tourniquet strapped to the stump that was once his arm.

As the Gusher walked into the room, Dooley glared angrily at his captor. "Hey, freak. Let me go," he said, pulling at his restraint. The Melonhead ignored him. Still fighting with his bonds, the enraged Chief croaked, "Hey, you ugly fuck. I'm talking to you!"

The Gusher turned and looked at Dooley. *Is that thing smirking at me?* he thought. "Cut me down, you piece of shit." He swung his stump. "At least give me a fighting chance."

The Gusher slowly walked toward Dooley. As he drew near, he pulled out a large handmade knife. Fluid squirted from the hose that was hanging from his deformed head.

Dooley saw the challenge. "Atta boy! Bring that blade here and cut me down," and then, under his breath, he muttered, "so I can kill you fuckers."

The Gusher moved in close, within inches of Dooley's face, and stared directly into his eyes, raising the blade and resting it on the rope around Dooley's neck.

"That's right, boy. Now just cut the rope."

The Gusher grinned and rubbed the blade against the rope. Dooley watched and waited. The Gusher sliced a tiny bit of the bond away... and then stopped.

"Don't stop! Keep going!" Dooley spit as he spoke. "C'mon, you freak!"

The Gusher pulled the knife from the rope. "What the hell are you—" but before he could finish his sentence, the Gusher raised a hand and put his dirty finger to Dooley's lips, stifling the rest of his words.

"Shhhhhhh, Eddie" the Gusher said. "Shhhhhhhh."

As the Gusher hissed Dooley's name, he plunged the jagged blade into Dooley's stomach, dragging it along the length of his body. Blood spurt from Dooley's mouth as his intestines spilled from the gaping wound.

"You pussy," Dooley muttered, his words muted by the blood, but death did not take him—yet.

As Dooley hung there bleeding, the haggard Skank Melonhead crept into the room where the Gusher was tormenting Dooley. He saw her come in, and in what could have been interpreted as some sort of 'apology' for killing her baby, seemed to 'offer' Chief Dooley to her. Her eyes widened at the sight of the freshly disemboweled Dooley, as she scampered toward him.

The Gusher watched for a moment and then left the room, moving on to the next chamber of the cave, as Skank started eating the still-alive Dooley! As Dooley's last bit of life left him, he mustered enough strength to leave the Gusher with one final jab.

"Burn in hell, pussy!" he said to the exiting Gusher.

The last thing Eddie Dooley saw as he died was the Skank Melonhead enjoying her 'meal'.

CHAPTER TWENTY-ONE

Doug Bryant's annual Backyard Tiki Bar Party was hopping. It was filled with fellow teachers from Kirtland High as well as most of the locals. As usual, the yard was decorated with tiki torches—citronella oil to keep those damn mosquitoes away—as well as Chinese lanterns and a huge fountain spurting blue water, its colored LED lighting adding a jovial accent to the water streams.

All along the Doug's custom-built hand-crafted (he made sure to remind EVERYONE that it was 'custom built' and 'hand crafted') tiki bar, coconuts and pineapples hung with reckless abandon, adorning almost every inch of 'unoccupied' space. There was a band playing in a large corner of the deck, where, this year, Doug had built a stage.

Mac and Susan heard the music as they pulled onto the street and they both smiled.

Doug spotted them as they walked up the driveway. "Hey Coach! Glad you could make it!" he said, happily. He was already on his third pina colada, probably his fourth, judging by the alcohol-smelling stain on his Hawaiian shirt.

"Thanks, Doug," said Mac, as he gestured toward Susan. "You know Doctor Reilly."

Doug's red eyes widened. "Oh! Hi!" He turned and pointed to the crowd of merry-makers. "Now we have TWO Doc Reillys here." Mac and Susan smiled as

Doug's red-rimmed eyes focused on the barbecue, where the elder Doc Reilly and Otis, the fellow from Smitty's Barber Shop, were chatting. "I guess we're in good hands if someone gets sick."

"It's nice meeting you, Doug," she said, and then turned to Mac. "I'm gonna go talk to my Grandfather for a minute."

"Sure," Mac replied, as Susan turned and walked toward Reilly and Otis at the barbecue. Mac watched her as she walked away and smiled, when suddenly Doug grabbed him by the arm.

"Coach," he said, he fruity breath causing Mac to squint slightly. "I want to show you something." Mac tried to resist, but could only shrug as Doug pulled him away.

As Mac was being 'kidnapped', Susan walked up behind her grandfather, and gave him a little kiss on the cheek.

"Hello, my dear!" he said with happy surprise.

"Hi, Grandpa." He smiled as she put her arm around his waist and gave her a kiss on the forehead.

Otis smiled. "It sure was nice talking to ya, Doc," he said to the elder Doc Reilly. "I'll leave you with your granddaughter."

As Otis shook his hand, Reilly said, "The pleasure was all mine Otis. And tell Smitty I agree with you. Pelé was a better guard than Doctor J."

Susan threw her grandfather a '*what the hell are you talking about?*' look as Otis smiled and walked away, making a bee-line to Smitty, who was enjoying a large umbrella-clad cocktail.

"Pelé played in the NBA?" she coyly asked with a wink.

"It drives Smitty crazy," and then added teasingly, "Anymore Melonhead sightings?"

She smiled. "No. Clear forecast for the day. Not a Melonhead in the sky." She laughed as he patted her leg.

"Good to hear, pumpkin," he said as they turned their attention to the party.

Doug dragged Mac to the far end of the party and made a grand gesture. All along the outside of the roof of the tiki bar, a toy train ran, each car holding eight cans of beer. "It's a train, Coach!" Doug exclaimed, his face aglow with excitement. "Can you believe it? A beer train!"

"That's pretty amazing, Doug," Mac said, watching the train make its 'deliveries'.

"I call it the 'Brew Choo-Choo'."

"That's pure genius," Mac said, not hiding the patronizing tone.

***

This is embarrassing, thought Johnny, as he pulled out of the garage on his bicycle, adorned in a Hawaiian shirt and khaki pants. *He COULD have waited for me.* He didn't know how to feel, his father being out on a date, but what could he do? His mother had walked out without a word, not even calling on his birthday or any of the holidays. As he peddled off down the street, he shouted to no one in particular, "Woo-Hoo! Tiki party."

Little did Johnny know was that someone—some THING—was watching.

***

From the woods near his house, the Gusher, along with several other Melonheads, watched as Johnny left his house and headed to Doug Bryant's Tiki Bar Party.

***

As Susan left Reilly to find Mac, who was still at the end of the bar with Doug, she passed Otis, who was chatting with a scantily-clad young woman sipping from a long-neck beer bottle. As she walked by, she couldn't help but smile as she overheard Otis say, "...and I told Smitty Pelé played in the NBA."

She looked at Mac as she got closer and he had a *please help me* look on his face. Doug was dominating the conversation, his histrionics visible from across the street. As she got closer, she caught the tail end of what Doug was saying.

"If you think that's cool," he said, spittle spraying, "wait 'til you see what I did next."

The little train was making its rounds and Doug pointed. "Filled the last car up with those little bottles of whiskey you get on an airplane."

Mac feigned surprise. "Wow."

Doug continued, unfettered. "And I call that... the 'Cabooze'! He laughed drunkenly at his own pun. "Get it? Ca-BOOZE!" He thumped Mac on the arm as the band began to play a slow song.

Time to play the hero, Susan thought as she deftly interrupted Doug's rambling. "Hey, Coach," she said as she glided next to him. "You feel like dancing?"

"No," he replied in mock seriousness, "but I'm sure Doug here wouldn't mind." The look on Susan's face showed a SEVERE lack of amusement, to which Mac quickly said, "I'm just messing with you. Of course, I would."

He turned to Doug. "Sorry, Doug," leaving Doug with his drink and his train.

As they walked away to dance, Doug's eagle eye caught a situation developing across the yard that needed his attention straight away.

"Harvey!" he called out as he walked. "Get that out of the dip! That's not an ointment."

***

As Johnny zipped along Wisner Road on his bicycle, his pant leg suddenly got caught up in the chain, binding itself in the derailleur. Johnny glanced down, making sure he retained control of the bike, and glided off to the side of the road to free his trapped trouser. As he bent to turn the pedals backwards to release the fabric, he began muttering. "I'm in a hurry," he said, mocking his father's tone. "Take the bike." He struggled in vain to ease his pant leg out of the gears.

From the woods, the Gusher and the group of Melonheads watched Johnny in his struggle with the chain. As he pulled again at his pant leg, he said out loud, "Great." He sighed with contempt, angry at his father, and sat up straight on his seat. "That's not coming out."

And then he heard them.

Johnny turned quickly to find the Gusher, flanked by several other formidable-looking Melonheads, leap out of the woods. One of them was much larger than the rest, even larger than the Gusher. As they all moved slowly toward Johnny, the Gusher patted the gargantuan Melonhead and pointed at Johnny. Johnny's mind raced with fear as he jerked frantically at his pant leg.

The group of Melonheads stopped, with the exception of the behemoth Melonhead, who continued to shamble toward Johnny.

A sudden surge of adrenaline shot through him as Johnny mustered enough strength to tear his pant leg free from the gears. As the thing drew nearer, he leaped back onto his bicycle and pedaled away as fast as he could. The quick move surprised the Melonheads, but the giant one (*the Goliath-looking one,* thought Johnny) that was stalking him charged behind him, closing the gap between them.

***

As others at the party began to fill the dance floor, Mac and Susan made their way to the middle of the floor. Mac took Susan's right hand, and put his right hand on her hip. "You a good dancer?" he asked, trying to use his best Fred Astaire moves.

'Sure," Susan replied smiling, "but you won't keep up if you take yourself too seriously."

"You think I take myself too seriously?" Mac said with mock indignation.

Susan was serious. "I think you worry too much about what other people think of you instead of what makes you happy."

Mac thought for a second before responding. "How's that?"

"Well," she began, "what people expect of you. I don't think you quite know how to handle being here with me." She glanced around the room. "Judging eyes, the gossip of a small town." She paused and looked him in the eyes. "Your reputation."

Mac also looked around the room. "Well, isn't that anybody on any date? Not knowing exactly what to do? Being nervous?"

Susan rested her head on his shoulder. "Okay," she said with a smile. "We can call it a date if you want to."

The look on Mac's face said it all. *I REALLY stuck my foot in my mouth this time.*

"I think you beat up on yourself too much," she continued. "You got a lot going on in there," she said, patting his chest. "But you're missing the best parts of yourself."

Mac winced as she realized she touched a raw nerve within him. He tried to turn away, to put up that wall, to block out everything. He turned to look at her… and she was looking at him, looking practically INTO him, and was smiling. "You know what I think, Mac?"

"No," Mac replied, feeling more at ease than he had in a long time, "but that's kind of the fun of it, isn't it? Gettin' to know somebody." He smiled.

"That's a good answer, Coach," she said with a twinkle in her eye and a little-girl giggle in her voice. "Good, answer." She squeezed him tighter, resting her head on his barrel chest. *He's such a teddy bear*, she thought as she closed her eyes and they continued dancing—dancing as if they were the only ones in the room.

***

Johnny knew without turning (he didn't DARE to turn) that the Goliath Melonhead was gaining on him. He pedalled faster, knowing that his life literally depended on it, hoping his leg wouldn't cramp. Images of Tony flashed through his mind. *I wonder if this is how HE felt*, Johnny thought, as he rounded a curve.

He saw Doug Bryant's house just a few yards ahead.

***

Ol' Doc Reilly stood at the edge of the dance floor, grinning from ear to ear. He hadn't seen his granddaughter this happy in a long time. *She hasn't smiled like that since she got her PhD*, he thought. *She had once said that she hoped she would be as good a doctor as he was. She's better.* He watched as Susan and Mac danced, moving with the rhythm of the music, lost in each other's arms. The fact is he hadn't seen MAC this happy in a long time. Mac hadn't smiled—GENUINELY smile—since Eva left. If there were two people who deserved to be happy...

Suddenly, Johnny fell from the top of Doug's fence, crashing down onto the band's drum set, sending cymbals and stands flying, knocking the tom-toms off the kick drum, and pushing the drummer off the stool. Everyone at the party was startled at the sudden commotion. Johnny jumped up and raced toward his father, as Mac stared at him in embarrassment and disbelief.

"Johnny!" he yelled. "What the hell are you doing?!"

As Johnny ran to his father, he breathlessly cried, "That thing is chasing me!"

Mac was flustered. "What thing?" he said angrily as he marched toward Johnny. Suddenly, the Goliath Melonhead burst through the fence, sending wood planks and splinters flying into the crowd.

"THAT thing!"

Mac stood and stared in shock and amazement. *Johnny was telling me the truth*, he thought, just as one of band members ended up being too close to the Melonhead was violently backhanded and launched across the yard. Panic ensued. The band abandoned their instruments and ran off as everyone at the party shrieked and ran from the intruder.

Everyone, with the exception of one person.

As the floor cleared of party-goers, the elder Doc Reilly stood alone.

The Goliath Melonhead stopped and looked as Doc Reilly marched toward him. "Stop!" he yelled at the beast. "You're not wanted here. Go back to woods with the others. Go back to your cave." The Goliath Melonhead stood there with what could be perceived as a confused look on its distorted face.

Mac didn't know what to do. "What is he doing?" whispered.

Susan became frantic. "Grandpa, get away from him!"

Reilly remained calm. "Don't worry, my dear," he said in a soothing tone. "I know how to handle this one." He continued marching right up to the beast, his face practically at the center of its chest. "You heard me. Get out of here."

The Melonhead stood there, squinting at Reilly as he reached into his pocket and pulled out a butterscotch hard candy and handed it to the Goliath.

"See Coach?" whispered Otis from behind a table. "I told you they like candy."

As the Melonhead took the candy, Reilly said, "Now go!" and poked it in the chest in an attempt to make himself the dominant aggressor in this situation.

Unfortunately, that little bit of assertiveness was all it took to set off the Goliath, which had another agenda in mind. It grabbed Old Doc Reilly and lifted him. With its large, distorted mouth it bit into Reilly's shoulder and clavicle, tearing flesh and shattering bone, and sending spurts of blood everywhere. As Reilly realized too late his mistake, the Goliath whipped him against the fence like a life-sized rag doll. As he crumbled to the ground, Susan raced over to help, and the Goliath refocused his attention on his original target—Johnny Gordon.

Mac saw the look in its eyes. *Not MY son*, he thought as he jumped between Johnny and that monstrosity. "Don't even think about it," he growled at Johnny's attacker. The Goliath Melonhead just sneered, almost mocking Mac, and charged, barreling toward him like a locomotive.

Mac's years of football training and coaching kicked in. Mac lowered his head a charged likewise at the beast like a football tackle, crashing into the Goliath's waist—with NO effect! Mac was a bit dazed after the impact, but felt the full effect of the Goliath's log of a forearm drop onto the middle of his back, crumbling him to the ground in a heap.

Mac quickly regained his senses and sprang up, punching the Goliath Melonhead, first in the stomach and then square in its warped face. *It barely flinched!* Mac thought as the beast rocketed a fist past Mac's face, which he crouched to avoid just in time.

Foregoing any Marquise de Queensbury rules of boxing, Mac landed a series of jabs into the thing's midsection and kidneys, but a swift uppercut from the monster sent Mac flying to the ground. Mac clenched his jaw and struggled to regain his senses and get back up on his feet. As he got to his knees, the Goliath marched over to Mac in what looked like triumph, looking to land the killing blow.

A moment of extreme clarity dawned on Mac as he looked up from his kneeling position, and stared directly into the beast's crotch. *I don't care WHAT species you are* Mac thought, as he drew his arm back and unleashed the hardest straight punch he ever threw—right into the Goliath's testicles. The Goliath reeled back, clutching his groin, a pained expression crossing his face, his misshapen eyes crossing.

Mac backed away while he had a chance, but Goliath quickly shook off the attack. He glared at Mac, obviously angry.

"Oh, crap," Mac said out loud.

The Goliath grabbed Mac and hurled him into the tiki bar, smashing glasses and bottles, and knocking the train off the rails. Suddenly, Doug popped out from behind a lawn chair. "No!" he cried, witnessing the destruction. "Not my train!"

The Goliath wasted no time after ridding himself of the pesky 'distraction'. He scanned the yard and spotted Johnny.

But that pause for the scan was just enough time for Mac to regain his composure and footing and charge the Goliath again. "Ahhhhhhhh!" he screamed as he raced to meet his foe, only to be grabbed up by the neck. The Goliath lifted him easily off the ground, both hands around his neck squeezing. *Is he giggling at me*, thought Mac as the world around him grew hazy.

Then he heard someone whistle.

The Goliath turned to see Johnny standing about five yards away, holding a coconut that he had grabbed from a tropical fruit basket. As the beast loosened his grip on Mac and turned to fully face him, Johnny hurled the coconut like a perfect spiral (*like a fuckin' BULLET,* he used to say) and struck the Goliath right in the middle of his forehead with such force that it caved in his skull and stayed there, dropping the monstrosity. The Goliath Melonhead fell over like a mighty tree in a forest, crashing down, flattening two chairs.

Mac shook his head to clear it, but saw every second of the 'action'. "You really need to start playing football again," he quipped as he staggered to his feet.

Mac yanked a tiki torch out of the ground and walked over to the prone giant, and rammed the still-lit torch into the beast's chest and through his heart. The Goliath lurched forward and screamed, falling back down, dead. Mac leaned on the torch that was protruding from the monster's chest and turned toward Johnny, who ran up to him and hugged him. Both were still in shock. "I'm sorry I didn't believe you." Mac held onto his son, as if he was never going to let him go.

Susan was hunched over her grandfather. "Mac!" she called. He pulled away slightly from Johnny, looking toward her. Johnny loosened his grip on Mac and pushed him to go to her.

"How is he?" Mac asked, as he saw the gaping wound across Reilly's neck and shoulder pouting blood.

"He's losing a lot of blood," she said with no panic in her voice. "A LOT of blood." She quickly put her hand in her pocket and pulled out her keys and tossed them to Mac. "It's gonna take a while for an ambulance to get here," she said, remaining professional, "so run to my office and get my medical bag. It's sitting right next to my desk." After a quick thought, she added, "Oh! And some gauze. I'll stay here and try to control the bleeding."

"Alright," he answered quickly and took off with Johnny right beside him. She watched as the two men dashed off, focused on their mission, leaving her with her grandfather.

"Hang in there, old man," she whispered to him. "We'll get you patched up."

"Thank you, dear," Reilly whispered back, surprising Susan a little. She looked down at him. *He seems so frail*, she quickly thought, but quickly dismissed it.

"Grandpa," she said after a brief moment of thought. The events of the last few minutes—*it WAS only a few minutes*, she thought to herself—were reverberating loudly in her mind, "Why were you talking to that thing?"

Old Doc Reilly stared at her. *He seems frightened*, she thought. The truth was he WAS frightened, but not of dying.

He was frightened of telling his beloved granddaughter, the little girl who idolized him, the young woman who modeled her life of medicine after him, the woman, no, the DOCTOR before him, tending to him. "Honey," he began. "Do you think

Doctor Crowe did it on his own?" He closed his eyes, embarrassed.

"I thought you said—"

"Something that big," he continued, "he needed help. I was just a resident at the time and eager to move up the ranks." Susan saw the look of shame on his face.

"Oh, Grandpa," she said, and leaned down and kissed his forehead, knowing that even her grandfather had flaws, and that everything could be forgiven and made better.

"It was the most radical idea I'd ever heard of," he continued. "Taking 'God's Mistakes' and changing their genetic and chemical makeup." His eyes lit up as he spoke. "Making them stronger. Healthier." He became pensive. "But I was wrong." He shook his head and winced at the pain. "The things he was doing..." He closed his eyes at the painful memory. "God! I can't even imagine."

The words seemed to leave a bad taste in his mouth, "...made them faster, stronger, more vicious than a normal human. He made them animals." He paused, knowing that there was nothing he could say that would justify his transgressions of half a century ago. "And I... I fixed the paperwork at the clinic."

He opened his eyes wide and looked right into her eyes. "I never touched them, pumpkin, I swear. But I made those children disappear. I helped make them not exist."

From outside the smashed fence, the Gusher Melonhead, the LEADER of the clan of hydrocephalic mutants, and several members of his 'family' gazed in at the carnage. The Gusher's eyes fixated on Susan, who was hovering over and caring for her grandfather.

The Gusher watched.

And remembered…

CHAPTER TWENTY-TWO
Flashback, 1964

The young Melonhead watched as Marilyn hovered over one of his 'siblings' feeding him hot dogs she had made. She had laid them out on a silver platter and sliced them into easily-eaten pieces. She flitted about the laboratory, feeding all of the children an equal share of treats, and she always sang. *She has such a soothing voice*, the boy thought.

"Hush, little baby, don't say a word," she would sing, "Mama's gonna buy you a mockingbird." She would sing to each child as she carefully fed them. "And if that mockingbird don't sing, Mama's gonna buy you a diamond ring." When she got to the large Melonhead—*oh, how I HATE that word*, she would say—she noticed a horrible rash that had worked its way up his face and neck. "Oh, you poor thing," she said, leaning in closer. "That rash looks terrible." She tilted his giant head to the side and looked at the rash. "Does it itch?" she asked.

"Yes," he replied with what could have been a smile on his distorted face.

"I'll go upstairs and get some cream for that, okay?" She smiled at the boy, who returned it, and she darted off up the stairs. She returned a few minutes later with a jar of antibiotic ointment and went over to the boy and began applying it to the infected area. He closed his eyes and sighed with obvious relief, not only at the soothing effect of the ointment, but that she was applying it with something akin to affection.

Just then, Dr. Crowe arrived home and noisily came down the lab/cellar stairs, still in his coat. He stopped before reaching the last step, surprised to find his wife down there with the children. He seemed quite nervous, although Marilyn didn't notice.

But the young boy did.

"Hello, dear," he said, clearing his throat. "What are you doing down here?" He changed the direction of the conversation, trying to make it less like and interrogation. "How are my patients?" he asked with a fake smile.

"They're doing well," she replied excitedly. "Except for the older boy. He has a horrible rash on his neck. Don't worry," she added proudly. "I put some ointment on it for you like a good little nurse." She was happy to help.

Crowe's demeanor changed slightly. Marilyn didn't notice. But the young boy did. "You put a cream on his rash?!"

"Just something to stop the itching." Without warning, he jerked her by the arm, pulling her away from the 'children' into a quieter conversation. The young boy craned his neck and listened, becoming agitated by Crowe's handling of Marilyn.

"Did I TELL you it was alright to treat MY patients?" he whispered hoarsely into her face.

Marilyn became confused, almost frightened by his attitude.

"No," she replied.

"Then WHY are you doing it?" He gripped her tighter.

"I was just trying to help."

He was beginning to hurt her.

"That rash may be a result of some treatment I have given him." He let go of her, and she ran her fingers along the marks he left on her arm. The boy noticed them. "I can't check the results of that treatment if I come home and his rash is gone because you put some damn ointment on him!"

Marilyn was confused by his anger. "I'm sorry, Malcolm. I wasn't thinking."

Crowe huffed. "Of THAT I'm sure!"

With tears welling up in her eyes, Marilyn said, "Oh, Malcolm," and scrambled .up the cellar steps, sobbing. Crowe turned and locked eyes with the young boy, who just glared at him.

Crowe moved closer to the young boy strapped to the bed. "Looks like we'll have to work faster."

***

The Gusher continued to stare at Susan for a moment as his mind returned to the present, and then turned to his 'clan', and motioned them to Doug's back yard. Susan looked up in time to see the army of Melonheads rushing in and attacking the remaining party guests.

Then suddenly, a large shadow eclipsed the surrounding commotion, as the Gusher Melonhead walked up and stood over her.

CHAPTER TWENTY-THREE

Main Street was surprisingly quiet as Mac's pick-up screeched to a stop in front of the police station, being that most of the townsfolk were at Doug's tiki party. Johnny had the door open and had hopped out before Mac had it in PARK. Mac jumped out of the driver's seat and pitched Susan's keys over the top of the truck to Johnny. "Run over to Doc's and get her bag and the gauze," he said as he ran into the police station. "I'm gonna get these guys out to Doug's."

Johnny gave him a thumbs up and dashed across the street to the doctor's office. Mac burst through the police station doors only to find Blue, in uniform, frantic and alone, sitting at the reception desk, holding a radio. As Mac ran toward the desk, Blue spun his chair to face him.

"Not a good time, Coach," he said, his voice showing the panic in his eyes.

Mac looked around the room and toward the back. "Where is everybody?" he asked.

"Out looking for Dooley."

Mac looked at Blue curiously. "Dooley?" He began to feel a twinge of concern. It wasn't like Chief Dooley to be out of touch to the point of having people actually have to look for him.

Blue became more frantic as he relayed the situation. "He went out looking for McClendon and

Claudio. He never came back, so now the deputies are searching the woods for him."

"No one's here?"

Blue shook his head. "Just me Coach."

The 'Coach Gordon' side of Mac suddenly kicked in. "Get them on the radio," he ordered. "There's been trouble at Doug's."

"I know!" cried Blue. "Everyone's been calling." He waved the police radio around in confusion. "I don't know what to do!"

Mac walked up to the desk and leaned in, practically hovering over Blue. "Just call them, Blue! Call 'em!"

Blue seemed to calm down now that he had direction. "Okay," he said, and hit the call button on the radio. "Vern," he said into the mic. "Come in." He was greeted by static. "Danny. Come in, Danny." Again nothing. He looked at Mac, his eyes growing panicky again. "That's weird. I just spoke to them an hour ago."

A sudden realization dawned on Mac. "Where are they looking?" he asked, already knowing the answer.

"The woods up by Wisner Road." That was the answer that Mac hoped he wasn't going to hear. He stood up straight as Blue looked at him, confused and silent.

"Blue," he said with deliberate clarity. "I need you to call County and get someone out here."

Blue looked almost insulted. "Coach, we got our own force," he said with some authority.

"Not anymore, you don't." Blue looked even more confused than before as Mac looked around the room and focused on the gun rack on the wall across the room. "You got the key to that gun rack?"

Blue shook his head as he jingled the keys on the desk. "I got keys to everything but that gun rack." He moved the keys out of his way and picked up the phone. As he dialed, he looked at Mac who was heading out the door. "What do I tell County we need 'em for?"

Mac's tone was brutally serious and foreboding. "Tell them the entire department is dead," and left, leaving Blue speechless and holding the phone.

The voice on the other end of the line saying "County, Officer McGee..." snapped Blue back to reality.

***

Johnny was waiting in the truck, holding Susan's bag and three packs of gauze. Mac jumped down the steps of the police station and into the pick-up.

"Did you tell them what happened?" Johnny asked, as Mac started the vehicle.

As he put the truck in DRIVE, he turned to his son and said, "There's no one left to tell," and sped off down Main Street back to Doug's.

Johnny just stared out at the road ahead.

They drove in silence as the headed toward Doug's and, as they pulled up to the house, the truck's high beams shone onto the damaged section of fence. "Dad," Johnny said as he focused on the fence. "It's broken in more than before."

Johnny was right. When they had left earlier, there was just one section blown out, but now half of the fence was completely destroyed. They pulled up onto the lawn and right up to the opening, allowing the headlights to light their way.

As they both got out of the truck, they were greeted by the most brutally gory carnage either had ever seen. Bodies—and body PARTS—lay strewn across the yard. Blood was splattered everywhere, and everything—tables, chairs, umbrellas, even the Brew Choo-Choo—was destroyed. It looked as if a psychotic tornado had focused on Doug's house and did it's worse. The only thing that was not destroyed was the fountain in the center of the yard, but even THAT was not untouched. Doug's mutilated body lay slumped over the lip of the fountain that had once been spouting beautiful crystal blue water. The fountain was now sprayed crimson, a brutal centerpiece of a nightmare vision.

A frantic looked crossed Mac's face as he scanned the area, looking at all the bodies, at all the carnage. "Susan!' he called out. His head turned and he spun around. "Susan!"

He began to run around the yard, hoping, PRAYING, that she wasn't part of this backyard abattoir. Then he heard a soft groan. He turned his head and saw the senior Doc Reilly, still alive, moving slightly, in the same spot where he had seen him before they left. Mac rushed over to him and knelt. "Doc," he said, confused. "What happened?"

Weakly, Reilly replied, "They took Susan."

Mac looked at Reilly, stunned.

"They didn't kill her. They just took her."

Knowing the answer, Mac asked anyway. "Where?"

Reilly knew what Mac was thinking. "There's too many of them. You'll never make it, Coach." He shuddered slightly and winced in pain.

"Watch me," Mac said, his anger becoming obvious.

"They'll tear you to shreds."

"Where?!" Mac demanded.

Reilly took a deep, gurgling breath. "Wisner," he whispered through a cough. "They took her to Wisner Woods." His head lolled slightly as he spoke. "Look for a hole or a soft spot in the ground. They have caves." Reilly began coughing hard. As he shifted, Mac noticed a huge pool of blood under him, growing wider. Mac looked back at Reilly, directly into his eyes.

"I'm gonna' have to leave you, Doc," he said with solemn resignation.

Reilly understood and smiled through the pain and growing darkness. "I know," he said, as Mac stood up to leave, still looking at him. "It's okay," he whispered. "I…" he coughed slightly, "I deserve this. Just save her."

As Mac began to walk away, Reilly reached out and caught Mac by the foot. "Coach."

"Yeah, Doc?" Mac knew this was the last thing Reilly would ever say.

"Arm yourself. You're gonna need it." Reilly looked at Mac with surprising clarity. "And go…" He coughed again. "Go for their heads."

The senior Doctor Reilly wheezed once more as his body grew tense. He shivered, and then his body relaxed as his eyes rolled back into his head, the light of life dissipating.

He was dead.

Mac stood over him. "Rest in peace," and then added with a shake of his head, "you stupid bastard."

CHAPTER TWENTY-FOUR

Susan drifted in and out of consciousness. The last thing she remembered before she blacked out completely at the party was this large creature with a leaking tube in its head and a slightly smaller thing wearing some kind of housecoat, much like her grandmother wore decades ago. As she came to, the thing in the housecoat was carrying her through some dark, muddy corridor. Here were a bunch of those things lurking in the shadows, eyeing her hungrily. *Oh, my God,* she thought. *I'm the next course!*

As she was being marched through a labyrinthine maze of tunnels, she tried to remember an escape route in case she got the opportunity to run, which, at this moment, seemed highly unlikely. They walked through a large archway, crudely dug out of the muddy walls, into a huge, cathedral-like 'hall', where about ten of those things—Melonheads—were milling around. Some were eating—*MY GOD!*, she thought—some sort of raw meat. Being a doctor, she recognized the 'cuts' they were holding, and the knowledge of what it probably was made her more than a little uneasy.

She felt her 'ride' slowing, as she was dropped unceremoniously to the muddy earthen floor. As she hit the ground and rolled, her supply of butterscotch candies rolled from her pocket and scattered across the floor. She quickly looked up and noticed that every Melonhead eye was looking in her direction. Not at her, though, but at the stash of candy. As she looked around the room, their gaze shifted from one 'treat' to the other—HER.

This is it, she thought as she lifted herself from the ground and got into a fighting stance she learned some years back in a martial arts course she had taken. Her grandfather had rather insisted she learn self-defense. *Had he foreseen this?*

As she crouched in readiness, a Melonhead, slightly more mutant-looking than the rest (*how much MORE mutant-looking could they get?* she mused) sprung from his corner and lunged at her, his conical teeth aimed right at her face. *I'm a goner,* she thought, when suddenly the thing was stopped mid-leap, inches from her face. The Gusher Melonhead had grabbed the other one by the throat, but his teeth were still snapping at her, looking for the opportunity to get a meal. The Gusher easily launched the other Melonhead across the room, slamming him into a far wall. The mob of Melonheads watched as the attacking Melonhead picked himself up and walked to the center of the crowd, defeated.

The Gusher stood tall and looked at the others. "Get out!" he ordered, as Susan looked at him in surprise. *It TALKED*, she thought, as she watched the Melonheads scamper out of the room like frightened hyenas, leaving him alone with her.

She began to think the worse as she heard what she thought were babies crying from another room. It looked from her to the butterscotch candies scattered around on the ground, and then looked at her and tilted his head. The thing just stared at her.

He just stared.

And remembered.

CHAPTER TWENTY-FIVE

The large young Melonhead watched Dr. Malcolm Crowe make his slow way through the lab, walking between the beds of captive Melonhead children towards a work table covered with specialized medical equipment—hoses and tubes and whatnot. (Most of the equipment adorning the table seemed rather arcane, definitely not stuff one routinely found in regular laboratories.)

The young Melonhead's eyes nervously tracked Dr. Crowe, measuring time by the sound of his foot steps. Tap. Tap. Tap, the noise hard on the white tiles, eerily ambient in the metal-filled lab. His heart beat nervously. Somehow, he knew the 'evil' scientist was up to no good. *Oh, where is Marilyn?* His mind flailed to the comfort of the beautiful woman who gave them candy.

He wasn't the only one watching. The other children were also awake, their eyes filled with terror. On those few times when his thoughts were coherent and linear, the Melonhead wondered how it was that the evil man never sensed their anger and hatred. It filled their air like hungry gnats, but the man was seeming insensitive, obtuse to anything other than his own dark purpose.

At that moment, almost like he felt his 'project's' scared eyes on him, Crowe paused his motion for a brief moment and looked over at the freakish child bound to the table, its huge head like a fishbowl, it's eyes misshapen gray goldfish. He smiled. The child cringed at that thin curl of Crowe's lips. All the children feared that smile—it spoke of deep mischief, was prophetic of bad fortune about heading their way.

Crowe turned away, reached the table. Shortly, sharp sounds came from that area of the room. The young Melonhead stared at Crowe's back, wondering what he was up to. As far as their bonds allowed, the other children's eyes were also focused that way. The noises grew sharper, louder, more insistent. They were strident and staccato, like a recording of crickets with parts erased in between.

Finally, Crowe turned around. He wasn't looking their way—was frowning, examining a long rubber hose with a sharp point at one end. Clearly what he'd just been working on. He looked up, his gaze slowly floating over the table to settle on the young Melonhead. The child watched in fear and confusion. He could tell that Crowe was measuring him, but for what?

Then Crowe nodded and grunted, "Yeah, it should fit you just right. Heaven knows your cranium's big enough."

Having made up his mind, he walked back across the room, his eyes now never leaving those of the young Melonhead, though his free hand strayed to touch those children on his left, all of whom flinched at the contact.

As Crowe drew closer, the young Melonhead's eyes darted left and right. He began hoping, PRAYING that someone (Maybe the Nice Woman?) would rescue him.

For a moment it even seemed his prayers might have been answered. Crowe, lost in thought, stopped his progress yet again, this time turning towards several cabinets to the left of the young Melonhead. Each cabinet bore several glass containers, most of which had 'Danger' death's head symbols on their bold labels. For a long while, Crowe stood there staring the cabinets, musing, his eyes almost glazed over.

(The young Melonhead couldn't read: In this case it was a mercy that he had no idea what those glass containers held. The knowledge would have confirmed his impression of Crowe as an evil man. The glass bottles held mixtures of steroids, Agent Orange, even a form of the 'white plague'—tuberculosis—graced the shelves of Crowe's medicine cabinet.

Crowe, a prisoner of the delusions of the typical scientific misanthrope, had been injecting each child with different combinations of his chemical concoctions and sloppily taking notes on his observations. His distance from reality was emphasized, nay confirmed, by his ignoring the fact that no established and respectable medical institution would ever accept his findings. He felt impelled to conduct his research, and medical ethics be damned. *Too radical they'll say*, he thought with a grin. *But so what, I'll show THEM*. Crowe acknowledged that genius such as his was never appreciated in its own time. This knowledge didn't deter him in the least. Now if Marilyn only understood this too . . .)

Shrugging with something almost like despondence in demeanor, the scientist pulling himself away from staring at the bottles and returned his attention to the work at hand. He walked quickly now, a sense of purpose in his eyes over the young deformed boy strapped helplessly to the bed, and bent over him.

The young Melonhead stared up at the man hovering over him. There was something almost like pity in Crowe's eyes as he regarded the sharpened tube.

"N-n-n-no," the boy blubbered, flailing in confusion, scared out of his mind.

Crowe reached down and clamped his hand over the boy's mouth, stifling his screams. Then slowly, his eyes now cold, he jammed the sharpened end of the hose into the shaved side of the boy's head at a point that had a circle with an 'x' drawn to indicate a lack of skull bone.

Blood and water flowed. The young Melonhead thrashed with pain. Crowe held him down fast on the bed and worked the tube in deeper. His lips were pressed tight with intense concentration.

The other children held captive in the lab stared and moaned in terror, their eyes almost popping from their faces in their fear.

The boy's consciousness faded with the pain...

CHAPTER TWENTY-SIX

The Gusher Melonhead looked down at Susan, his attention once again drawn to the candies. Fluid drizzled from the tube in his head. He looked up from the sweets, his weird eyes focusing completely on Susan.

He reached out a hand towards her. Seeing this, she closed her eyes, not knowing what was going to happen, especially after seeing what the other Melonheads were eating. Human flesh—it shocked her to the marrow that these creatures were cannibals. She was a captive in a den of cannibals?

Instead of the worst, though, the Gushing Melonhead touched Susan's hair, stroked it lovingly. He ran his fingers along her cheek and touched her lips as more fluid drained from the hose. "Mama," he said.

***

Mac's pick-up screeched to a halt in front of the school. He bolted up the stairs, automatically finding the key that unlocked the doors, and raced to his office, straight to the 'weapons locker', and whipped it open. He looked over the array of weapons accumulated over his tenure as shop teacher, amazed at some of the quality of workmanship.

Enough of that, he thought. *There's work to do*, as he reached behind his desk and pulled a large duffel bag. He began stuffing it full of any weapon that would fit in it, and some that didn't, he hung from his shoulder from straps that the students had thoughtfully designed into their projects.

The 'inventory' included machetes, ninja throwing stars, nunchucks, even a crude battle axe, and three swords were slung over his shoulder. As an afterthought, he grabbed a pack of cigarettes and a Zippo lighter he had just confiscated from a student two days prior. He slammed the locker closed and grabbed his flashlight before racing out the door and back into his vehicle.

***

Susan opened her eyes and watched as the Gusher Melonhead stroked her face, his thoughts obviously lost somewhere else. *At least he's not EATING me,* she thought, as she remembered the longing glance at the candies. She slowly pulled away from him, but before he could protest (attack?), she reached down and picked up some of the candies. He watched as she unwrapped one of them, and moved closer, his mouth opening slightly. She reached out and dropped the candy onto his waiting mouth. *He's like a little puppy getting treats,* she thought, as he closed his mouth. She heard sucking noises as he enjoyed the butterscotch candy, his eyes rolled back.

As the flavor of the candy washed over his tongue, he closed his eyes and smiled.

CHAPTER TWENTY-SEVEN

As the young Melonhead, now with a large tube sticking out from the side of his head, lay strapped to his bed, he heard pounding on the door at the top of the stairs. After several seconds, the pounding stopped, followed by light footsteps leading away from the door. A moment later, the footsteps returned. After a time of silence—a long duration punctuated by odd scraping and tapping, and some heavy breathing,—he heard a sudden crash, and next saw the cellar door come sliding down the steps. He looked up to see Marilyn climbing down the stairs.

***

Marilyn Crowe hadn't been downstairs for a week since her last discussion with her husband. A quiet, retiring woman, one who did her best to avoid conflict with her rather pushy spouse, she'd been cowed almost completely by his treatment of her over her use of ointment on his young charges.

But… in all those days when she'd not physically visited her husband's lab, her conscience had ridden roughshod on her. Each time she passed the door to the cellar, she'd first stiffen involuntarily, then quicken her paces, scampering away like a mouse that sensed a cat close by. There were no sounds, but Marilyn imagined she could hear the children screaming for her in their confused ways, or moaning in pain, while their eyes stared terrified from their grossly malformed craniums.

They're just kids! she repeatedly told herself angrily. *Deformed or not, they're human beings, not monsters. Their being that way is through no fault of their own! What if Malcolm and I had had a child and it turned out like one of them? What then? Would I blithely sit back and let my scientist husband experiment on it? Oh, hell no, I most definitely wouldn't...*

The thoughts steamed in her head, pound fiercely on the walls of her mind. She did nothing as first, however, reasoning: *It is science, after all, I don't really understand it too much, but I know Malcolm isn't a bad man, or else I wouldn't love him, and he is trying to help these kids...*

If Marilyn and Dr. Crowe had had kids of their own, Marilyn would likely not have dwelt on those downstairs (she'd have been able to view them as dispassionately as her husband did), but now, she and her husband's lack of any children of their own made Marilyn particularly conscious of the ones trapped down in the basement laboratory. The children, deformed as they were, called to her maternal instincts.

During the time since his reprimanding her, Malcolm himself was cordial, very loving even, in his distracted way. He joked with her constantly, complimented her on her looks, even bought her a gift of chocolate, something he'd not done in a while.

They discussed his work each evening (usually at dinner) when he returned from the cellar, locking the door behind him.

"How is your work going, darling?" she asked dutifully over their plates of grilled fish garnished with lemon.

"Not bad," he'd grunt noncommittally. "Could be much better though. They're not responding to treatment fast enough. I'm starting to worry now that I can't help them."

"You're starting them on a new course of drugs?"

"Yes, the last combo was useless. So now I'm trying another approach: a calculated mix of steroids; something to enhance fluid drainage from their lateral cranial fiss—" He grinned apologetically at her between sips of water, "Sorry, honey, I mean from the side of their skulls…"

She smiled back genially. "I understand the scientific jargon, dear. I've been married to you for long enough now."

"Thanks, darling," he beamed back. "You've no idea how much it means to me that you're so understanding." He drank more water, cut off a slice of fish, and popped it into his mouth. After chewing and swallowing, he added: "Don't get me wrong, Marilyn: I don't at all doubt that I'll crack this—these new enhancing drugs are certain to work . . . oh, I'm certain of their effectiveness in the long term, this is just a minor setback . . ." he frowned at his plate as if the filleted fish that lay on it held the secrets of all life in the universe and was withholding it from him, "but it's just frustrating not knowing the proper mix of drugs. I mean I want a cure right now."

Marilyn's eyes widened. "A cure? But, Malcolm, hydrocephaly is congenital, surely..."

He laughed. "Yes, I know, I know... I know the conventional wisdom. I pay lip service to it myself amongst my colleagues." Speaking next Dr. Malcolm Crowe's voice rose both in volume and pitch in a combination of sudden impatience and vexation: "'DNA research is the key... we need to rewrite the genetic code,' we keep saying; but for how long? How long are we going to hope for a breakthrough that might be a century in coming, while all the while..." he made an expansive gesture with his fork which Marilyn recognized as encompassing their basement, "just how long do we wait? And meanwhile (another broad gesture)... meanwhile tons of innocent children suffer through no fault of their own..."

"But a cure?" Marilyn persisted. She was glad of this discussion with him. It felt like he was involving her again in his work, like her faux pas with the ointment of a few days ago no longer counted. Of course, she didn't intend going back down into the cellar again for a while, but... She noticed he was frowning again, hoped his anger wasn't directed at her seeming to doubt his capability to solve the problem. "What I mean, darling, is... how do you cure something like a hydrocephaly?"

Condescending anger ruled Dr. Crowe's features for a moment, then he smiled. "I understand, dear. I mean rather to manage the condition. If I can somehow shrink the head size of the sufferer, reduced the pressure of water on the infant brain… drain the excess off, and stimulate the missing tissue to grow up in its place…" His eyes gleamed at her, he reached across the table, held her hands. "Just imagine, Marilyn, what an improvement it would be in their lives, what an enhancement it would be…"

And listening to him then, Marilyn Crowe felt a rush of joy in her breasts, a gladness that her husband was truly committed to making a change in society, that her doubts about him were all wrong, that he really was a good man. A very good man. And she gripped his hands hard and stared at him lovingly, her mind at peace.

But later, after she'd done the dishes, while Malcolm was reading a newspaper, Marilyn sat staring at the muted living-room TV lost in thought. Now her euphoria over her husband's good intentions had worn off. She was worried, something about Malcolm's glib replies, his intense 'honestly' to do good… his intention to 'enhance' the children didn't ring quite true. Replaying their dinner conversation in her mind, she pinpointed her fears on that exact word: enhance. It struck her just the wrong way.

She surfaced from her thoughts, gazed at her husband. "Darling?"

He regarded her over the financial section. "Yes, honey?"

"I'm just remembering what we discussed at dinner. About the kids downstairs?"

He wagged a finger at her in reprimand. "Try to think of them as test subjects, Marilyn. I keep telling you how it's best not to get too close to them emotionally, or else one might ignore the long-term benefits of our research for the short-term satisfaction of not causing them pain. As much as I dislike the term myself, they're really just guinea pigs, poor creatures suffering for science. I'm sorry there's no better description of their plight."

She nodded, too caught-up in her thoughts to be hurt by his patronizing attitude. "Yes, Malcom, whatever you say." She frowned. "What I was going to ask is: how certain are you that you'll be able to help these … test subjects? I mean how really, *really* certain are you?"

He looked for a moment like he was about to lose his temper. Then he laughed. "Oh, I'm very sure, I'll be able to enhance them."

Marilyn nodded demurely, her eyes flashing prettily at her husband's. Inside however she was now really bothered. *Okay, there's that word again: enhance.* Oh no, Malcolm, something's not right here. There's something about this project of yours that you're not telling me.

From that moment, Marilyn Crowe began wondering exactly what her husband was really up to in their cellar with the mutant children.

***

Marilyn didn't immediately do anything against her husband's wishes. For the whole of the next day she made up her mind. The door to the cellar stairs was kept permanently locked now, and Malcolm now kept the key on him, at least she couldn't find it anywhere in the house. So she knew he didn't trust her not to meddle in his affairs, so as they were.

So she spent that day thinking, considering whether to break in (and how would she do that?) or not. Four or five times she to the locked cream opening, pausing to pout thoughtfully at it. For some reason the hinges had been set outward in the lock, not inside it as was regular. *Oh, but the screws looked so big! Do we have a large-enough screwdriver at home?*

Each time, Marilyn would stare at the door for five minutes or so, gathering up her courage to trespass on her husband's research. Each time, she'd decide: *not now, later.*

So she passed the day. She did, however, after imagining she'd heard a whimper of pain from downstairs, hurry out to the garage and putter around amidst the shelves of tools there, at last coming away with a huge heavy star-tipped screwdriver which she instantly carried back inside and tested on the screws in the door hinges. The screwdriver was a perfect fit. Marilyn felt triumphant in her mental crusade. If she'd not yet acted; she'd made sufficient preparation to do so. All she needed now was to get her nerve up sufficiently to defy Malcolm.

She said nothing to her husband that night after dinner, was surprised when he mentioned it himself:

"Someone's coming in to replace the cellar door tomorrow, Marilyn."

"Oh." She looked up, surprised. "Why?" Her face tightened. "Malcolm, I'm not going down there again.

And you don't have to keep taking the key out of the house either."

He nodded. "I'm sorry about that, but I..." He abandoned the explanation. "There've been several break-ins this past week, just down the road. I'm sure you know what the consequences will be if some conscientious burglar discovers what's cooking in our basement."

She nodded, very flustered. Malcolm was obviously lying—there'd been no break-ins anywhere around. She was certain of that. Yesterday, when she'd visited the mall, there'd been no mentions of any burglaries.

Malcolm continued: "So I'm having Jory Crane— you remember him, don't you—drop by and replace the current wooden cellar door with a steel one." He absentmindedly tapped his chest pocket (where Marilyn imagined the cellar key currently resided). "Much safer for everyone, the children inclusive. (Marilyn detected a mocking accent on his pronunciation of 'children.') Just imagine if our burglar isn't so conscientious after all, but instead freaks out at the site of the kids."

Again she caught that mocking emphasis on 'kids.'

She didn't retort or question him. "Yes, darling, I agree," she replied demurely. Meanwhile her mind boiled over with planning. *Tomorrow? Damn, I have to get in there before Jory comes over. Now, I know for certain that Malcom's hiding something from me I really wonder what the hell it is now!*

Tomorrow couldn't come quickly enough.

After a nighttime of perfunctory lovemaking (she was way too worried to do more than fake an orgasm), burning the breakfast toast (something she never did) and distractedly kissing Malcolm goodbye at the front door (which he in turn seemed too distracted to notice), was finally left alone to execute her plans.

Marilyn waited for thirty minutes to ensure Malcolm wouldn't suddenly return to pick up some forgotten papers, then she grabbed up her screwdriver and rushed to attack the hinge screws.

Jory Crane wouldn't be here till 2 p.m. Marilyn smiled coolly as, standing on tip-toes, she poised the tool in the highest screw-head. That gave her more than enough time to get this done.

***

It took Marilyn half an hour to get all the screws out. Two of them were so stiff she had to lever them out of their holes by sticking the screwdriver under the hinge itself. Finally, though, she was done. She stood up panting, covered with sweat even though the morning was quite cool.

Impatient to enter the cellar, even though she felt fatigued and her knees ached from crouching for so long, she tried to pull the door out. It didn't come free easily, mainly because it was heavier than she expected. Levering it free of its frame with the screwdriver, she gripped it firmly around the edges and pulled. It came free grudgingly from the lock; then... either she slipped or the door did (she wasn't later certain which had happened), then door was suddenly out of her control and crashing and sliding down into the cellar.

Oops, Marilyn thought, as it smashed into the bottom of a cabinet, shattering a number of glass bottles. *Malcolm's gonna be furious.*

Realizing that there was now no chance of her concealing her intrusion into the lab, she firmed her resolve and stepped through the door and, holding the big screwdriver in front of her body like a weapon, quickly made her way down the stairs.

Once about halfway down the stairs and able to see the room clearly, Marilyn froze.

Now, standing poised on the middle steps, She was mortified by what she saw. The children were in horrifying states of abuse, their faces more distorted than before, and obviously not as a result of their hydrocephalic condition. Some were covered in rashes, some were even bleeding from their eyes and noses. And off in his in own area was her 'big boy,' now with a hose dangling from the side of his head.

She continued to the bottom of the stairs and slowly walked across the room. From his bed, the young Melonhead watched as she got closer. As she walked past Malcolm's desk, she glanced down and saw a folder with a U.S. Government seal emblazoned across the front.

She looked around the room before picking it up and opening it. "Chemical enhancement?" she muttered as she read the file. She turned and looked at the children, her face stern. "You don't look *enhanced* to me!" she boldly proclaimed to them.

Her attention focused on the large young Melonhead. "My God!" she cried as she ran over to him. She stopped right next to him and leaned over, this being the first time she saw what Malcolm—her HUSBAND—had done to the poor boy. His skin was riddled with blisters, and the hose that dangled from his head was attached to an IV bottle that fed straight into his head. She stared, and then ran her finger along the length of the tube, gently. She then turned and grabbed a chair and brought it next to him and sat. He looked up at her as she gently stroked his hand. "What has he done to you?" she said in a soothing voice. The young Melonhead moaned. He rose slightly, looking deep into her face.

"Candy?" he meekly asked. She looked at him in surprise. She frantically began searching her pockets, knowing that she had butterscotches on her somewhere, desperate to find them in a hurry, knowing that the candies were the only solace this poor boy would get right now. As she fumbled with her sweater pocket, she produced a handful. The young Melonhead lit up when he saw the prize.

"Is THIS what you want?" she asked, holding out her hand. She unwrapped one of the candies and dropped it into his open, waiting mouth. As she sat back, she noticed that the restraints hold him down were cutting into his wrists. She looked around the room for some kind of ointment, now with no regard to the reprimand she receive before. (This horror was too great to behold, all her husband's complaints paled to nothing before it.) Not finding any Candy, she turned back to the deformed boy and rubbed his hands, trying her best to soothe him. "Don't worry," she said, a tear working its way down her cheek. "It's gonna be alright."

The boy finished his candy and whispered, "Mama."

"What did you say?" She leaned closer to his face.

"Mama," he repeated.

"Yes." *I guess I AM his 'mama'*, she thought.

"Help me." Marilyn's eyes widened as she jerked back from him. "Help me!" he said again, a little louder. She slid back in her chair, away from the boy. He began screaming. "Help me!"

Marilyn became terrified. She quickly stood, knocking over the chair as she shuffled back. "HELP ME!" he cried again, as she turned and raced to the stairs, hopped over the fallen door and ran up the steps. The young Melonhead's head dropped back onto the bed, his eyes never leaving the stairway. "Help me, Mama," he whispered.

CHAPTER TWENTY EIGHT

The pick-up truck raced down Main Street toward Wisner Woods. Mac had heard of Dr. Crowe and the mansion over the years, and even saw some of the actual building before it succumbed to nature as he was growing up, but Johnny never knew about it, never knew about Melonheads or experiments. Mac didn't think Johnny knew there was even a structure within the woods.

They drove quickly, knowing that time wasn't on their side. As Mac pulled up to Wisner Woods, Johnny was practically out of the vehicle before it came to a complete stop. *Damn kid thinks he's indestructible*, Mac thought, and not without envy. Johnny was an athlete, physically fit, and a formidable opponent in any sports situation. Mac jumped out of the truck and ran to the other side, as Johnny pointed to a Kirtland P.D. squad car on the side of the road, one of its doors wide open, but no one inside.

Johnny ran over to the vehicle. "Dad!" he exclaimed, pointing at the side of the cruiser. There was blood smeared along the entire driver's side. Johnny slowed as Mac ran past him and peered inside.

His father had spied a shotgun locked to the dashboard and tried to pry it free. Johnny ran up to help Mac, but to no avail. As they stepped back away from the police cruiser, they watched and listened for anything strange.

"Keep your eyes open," Mac said quietly. "Let's go." He pulled a flashlight from the duffel bag and turned it on. They both headed into the dark woods.

***

The Gusher had fallen asleep. Susan had fed him several butterscotch candies over the last hour, as several other Melonheads walked past, eying them angrily. She now sat just a few feet from her captor as he snored, with fluid occasionally draining from the hose that was sticking out of his head. *What the hell is that thing?* she thought as she sat quietly on the ground, biding her time and waiting for an opportunity to sneak off and escape. She had been thinking of her grandfather and how he knew about these things, and how he kept his involvement with them secret all these years.

She looked around the room and back at the Gusher. She slowly rose to her feet, mindful not to bump into anything that was in this vast chamber. There was enough light for her to make out where the entrance was that she was brought in from and slowly and quietly tip-toed toward it. The corridor was bathed in shadow and as she drew near and was about to dash off to freedom, one of the Melonheads that had chased Tony Scicolone to his death appeared from the shadows, startling her. As she quickly whipped around to escape, she was confronted by the Gusher, who was standing directly behind her. He reached up and seized her by the throat, but, rather than crush the life out of her, he looked her in the eyes and wagged a scolding finger at her and sneered.

The other Melonhead moved closer as the Gusher released his grip on her, but stopped in his tracks as the Gusher glared at him. *My savior*, Susan thought with a hint of sarcasm.

***

Mac and Johnny walked through the woods, their eyes trying to see as much as the narrow beam of the flashlight would allow. *Damn! I should have looked for another flashlight in the police cruiser,* thought Mac as they tripped over fallen limbs. "Doc said to look for holes or soft spots in the ground," he whispered loudly to Johnny.

"Holes?" Johnny asked. "Soft spots? How the hell are we gonna find a soft…" and suddenly Johnny dropped into a 'soft spot' in the ground! He was barely able to cling to the edge as Mac ran up and hoisted him out. He had stumbled—literally—upon an entrance to the lair of the Melonheads!

"You were saying?" Mac mused as he shone the flashlight down the tunnel. The beam faded into the darkness, not finding a bottom. "That's spooky." He took a step backward and stumbled, falling to the ground.

Johnny jumped forward to try and catch him. "What are you doing?" he asked as he helped Mac to his feet.

"I tripped over something," replied Mac as he looked down and saw a large propane tank. *It's probably from McClendon's truck,* he thought.

"I have an idea," Mac said as he pulled a knife from his bag. He positioned the knife by the valve on the tank and, grabbing a rock, hammered it into the valve of the propane nozzle. He turned the knob and was greeted by a hissing noise and quickly turned it back. He turned to Johnny. "This is what I want you to do. Ten minutes after I go down there, I want you to open the valve on this thing and push it down the hole." Mac then reached into the duffel bag and grabbed the Zippo he had thrown in from the locker. He handed the rock and the Zippo to Johnny. "Wait one minute, tie your shirt around this rock, light it on fire, and then throw it down."

"Are you crazy?" Johnny exclaimed and shook his head. "No way!"

Mac was insistent. "Johnny. You have to."

Johnny continued to protest. "It'll kill you."

"Look, this can't be the only way in," Mac said, trying to be convincing. "There's got to be another way."

Johnny wouldn't listen. "What if there's not?"

Mac put a hand on Johnny's shoulder. "Then I'm probably already dead. And it's gonna' be up to YOU to blast the shit out of these evil bastards." He held out the rock and the lighter again.

"Dad," Johnny said, looking right into his father's face, "I don't want to." He was pleading but Mac was determined.

"I know," he said. "It's a bad spot I've put you in, but these things killed Tony and God knows who else." He looked down the hole. "And right now they've got Susan down there. Maybe she's still alive. And Johnny, I…" he paused, almost uncomfortable speaking to his son like this. "This is gonna' sound stupid, but this woman SAW me." He searched for the right words. "She understood a piece of me…and she smiled, Johnny."

Mac looked down and then back up to Johnny. "She didn't run away from all that guilt and regret and shit I've been putting myself through since your mother left." He swallowed hard, hoping that Johnny would see where he was coming from. "It's been a long time since somebody understood me." He sighed. "Even bothered to. That kind of person is worth saving." He looked down the hole again.

Johnny smiled. "I understand," he said.

Mac laughed, almost to himself. "I haven't even kissed her yet."

Johnny shook his head, still smiling. "Ten minutes?" he asked.

"That's right."

"Dad," Johnny began. "I'm sorry what I said about Mom. She loved you, and…"

"It's alright," Mac interrupted. "I love you. I'm proud to have you as my son. No matter what, remember that." He grabbed Johnny and embraced him, and then turned and jumped down the hole.

Johnny looked at his watch. It was exactly midnight. As he looked from his watch to the hole, Johnny thought, *You had BETTER come back.*

Mac slid down the muddy tunnel for what seemed like a quarter mile. *My ass is sore*, he thought as he scraped over rocks and twigs. He was finally spit out onto the cave floor with a dull thud. Coated in mud, he scanned the dimly-lit room, a light source from an adjoining tunnel the only illumination. As Mac rose to his feet and walked toward the light, he noticed, much to his surprise, several more propane containers in a chamber full of junk. "Oh, shit!" he said as he scurried back to the opening he had just fallen in from.

"Make it fifteen minutes," he shouted up the hole.

Not getting a response, Mac glanced down at the propane containers, and then noticed something near the entrance. His eyes focused and zeroed in on a wooden toboggan. *What the hell is a toboggan doing here?* he thought as he ran up to propane tanks and disabled them just as he did to the one above that Johnny was now tending to. He turned on all the valves, greet by a satisfying hissing sound from each of them. He ran over to the toboggan that was by the entrance and lifted it, blocking the opening. He smiled as the chamber began filling with gas.

Covering his face, he sprinted across the room and ran down the corridor that the illumination was coming from and discovered little campfires all over the ground.

"Great," he said out loud. "Good thinking with the gas." He looked up, following the smoke from the campfires as it climbed to the ceiling travelled along a consistent path. He remembered something from science class. "If there's a draft, there's a way out."

He saw that the smoke was flowing into an unlit area. *Perhaps a chamber where Susan was being held,* he hoped.

As he flicked on the flashlight, he was horrifically greeted by the dead and mutilated body of Chief Dooley! Mac stood at the entrance of the chamber, mortified, as the beam of the flashlight scanned the room.

He looked about the room and was shocked to find dozens, perhaps even HUNDREDS of eaten and decomposed bodies. *My God!* he thought. *This must be some kind of feeding room!*

Mac turned in a panic, but stumbled and fell. He landed face to face with the corpse of a woman. Before he could completely recoil away, he noticed something shiny—and familiar—around her neck. It was a heart-shaped locket with a tiny keyhole. As he stared in growing shock and disbelief, his lips began to tremble as tears welled up in his eyes. *No! It CAN'T be?!,* he thought, as he reached under his shirt and pulled the tiny key out that was hanging from the chain around his neck. He reached out with it and inserted it into the hole that was on the locket of the woman in front of him.

Mac felt himself become overwhelmed, a feeling of helplessness and loss, as his key fit perfectly into the locket around her neck. He did all he could to keep from completely losing his composure, but failed as he began to weep uncontrollably.

"I'm sorry, Eva," he cried, clutching the locket in his hand. "I'm sorry about everything." He touched the practically mummified remains of his wife. "You didn't deserve this." He took several deep breaths. "Everything you said was right. Johnny is fine." He tried to keep quiet, not knowing what danger lurked in the darkness, but he felt he HAD to speak. "I should have never pushed him so hard. If I would have listened to you, you'd still be with us." He grew determined. "I knew you didn't leave me. I knew..." He turned and looked over his shoulder. "I'm gonna kill every one of those fuckers." He stood, unsteady. "I'm killing them all."

He fell to his knees again, and buried his face in his hands and sobbed some more. He finally stopped and looked at his wife's remains one last time and composed himself. "Oh God!" he said out loud. "Susan."

Mac surveyed the room. Amongst the corpses, he found Claudio's corpse, still adorned in his maple-tapping apparel. He climbed over several bodies to get to his 'utility belt' and took the tree-tapping spikes. he turned to where Dooley lay and retrieved his 9mm Glock and the extra magazines. He put the pistol and the magazines in the duffel bag and attached the spikes to his belt.

Before leaving the chamber, he went back to his wife's corpse. He bent down and inserted the key once more into the locket around her neck and, this time, turned it. As he opened the locket, his lips tightened in anger as he saw a tiny photo of Johnny, Eva, and himself inside. "I gotta go, honey," he said to her. "I'll get those bastards for you." As he walked away, he turned one last time and said to Eva, "And you know me. I don't like to lose."

***

Johnny paced back and forth in front of the tunnel, his shirt tied around the rock. He must have looked at his watch a dozen times since Mac disappeared down the hole. Time dragged. It was 12:05. Dammit, he thought. Only five minutes. He didn't know what was worse; that only five minutes had passed or that he had to toss the flaming shirt down IN five minutes. he knelt down beside the edge of the hole. "Come on, Dad, he mumbled. "Come on, buddy." He choked back a sob as he looked at his watch again.

He was surprised at how worried he suddenly was about his father's wellbeing. It was a really strange feeling after all their years of subdued animosity.

***

Mac heard a strange mewling as he followed the tiny campfires along the corridor to another opening. As he entered the cavern, about a dozen baby Melonheads erupted into shrill screams from their earthen cradles scooped out of the muddy walls. Mac tried to blank out the sounds, hardly able to even look at the grotesque screaming little mutants. He dropped the duffel bag, reached in, and pulled out a large battle axe, compliments of Blake Logan, and hoisted it up into the air. He stepped up to the 'cradles' and was about to bring the axe down onto the tiny freaks, but suddenly stopped, practically in mid-swing.

He gazed down at them. They were just... children. Although they were freaks, they were still just children. As he slowly lowered the axe, the hag Skank Melonhead wandered in from an adjacent corridor. As she looked in on her babies, she saw Mac hovering above them, axe in hand, unaware of her presence.

He lowered his axe just as she charged in to defend them, screaming as she pounced on Mac, who had turned just in time to be tackled. The impact of Melonhead-on-human caused Mac to drop the axe and crash to the ground on his back, his head hitting with a resounding CRACK. The Skank Melonhead latched herself on top of him and snapped her cone-like teeth at him, inches from his face, and clawed at his head with dirty talon-like fingers.

Survival instinct took over as Mac thrust his forearm under her throat and yanked her off balance with his other hand. He quickly rolled away but barely got to his feet as the Skank slammed him into the wall.

Damn! She'd be a great tackle, Mac thought as his head pounded against the wall. As he crumbled to the ground, the Skank leaped on top of him and pummeled him, raining blows left and right. Mac did his best to block the attack as he fumbled for one of Claudio's tree-tapping spikes that he had secured to his belt. He managed to grab one with his left hand. He mustered all the strength he could with is right arm and forced the Skank's head up, and then reached over and stabbed her in the her bloated head.

Brain fluid spurted from the hole in the spike, showering Mac with hydrocephalic juice. The Skank listed to the side and wobbled, which allowed Mac to pull another spike from his belt and jab a second one into her cranium. As a second fountain of fluid erupted from that spike, the Skank's head began to shrivel, deflating like a leaking balloon. As Mac regained his footing, he ran to his fallen weapon and recovered his axe.

"Rule Number One," Mac growled. "ALWAYS protect your HEAD!" as he brought down the heavy weapon in a wide arc, neatly separated the Skank's head from the rest of her. As her head bounced across the floor, her body remained upright for a moment before it shook violently and collapsed to the ground.

A scream forced Mac to whip around quickly, where he saw a slightly smaller Melonhead, this one with the left side of his face and body swollen, deformed and distorted, racing toward him like a charging bull.

Instinctively, Mac threw the battle axe at the Lefty Melonhead, but missed horribly. He watched as it bounced noisily off the wall. "Shit," Mac said. "That always works in the movies."

Lefty looked at the fallen axe, smiled and picked it up. "Great. Just gave you my weapon." Mac snapped his fingers and smiled back at Lefty. "Except I've got…" He reached into the duffel bag as Lefty charged at him, axe raised, "BULLETS!"

Mac quickly drew Dooley's pistol and discharged the weapon, hitting the axe-wielding Lefty Melonhead directly in the forehead, the back of his head exploding in a rain of gore, and the creature dropped like a sack onto the muddy floor.

The sound of the 9mm reverberating throughout the underground Melonhead lair alerted all of them in every corner where they lurked. The Gusher wheeled around, his hose whipped and sprayed hydrocephalic fluid across the room, and sneered. Others congregated around him from adjoining chambers and corridors and awaited instructions. He looked at the gathering group and pointed toward the corridor leading to the 'nursery' where the gunshot sound originated, and they took off like a pack of wild beasts after the intruder.

Mac realized what he had done and scolded himself for not thinking about the consequences of the resulting noise from the gunshot. "You IDIOT!" he said aloud, but then shrugged. *Ahhh! What the hell*, he thought, as he lifted his head and shouted, "SUSAN! I'M COMING!" *They already heard the gunshot, so at this point, it doesn't matter, they know I'm here.*

The Melonheads weren't the only ones that heard the gunshot, and they weren't the only ones that heard him calling to Susan. His voice travelled throughout the cavernous Melonhead stronghold and into the very 'cathedral' where Susan was being held. She heard Mac's voice, faint but confident. Even in the face of imminent death by being eaten, she looked up and her face lit up. She smiled and thought, *someone's coming to save me!* But for Susan, it wasn't just someone. It was MAC who chose to rescue her. She trembled, but not with fear. A wave of courage ran through her like electricity as she responded to the voice of her savior, even as the Gusher charged into the room and began to tie her hands behind her back.

"MAC! I'M DOWN HERE!" she shouted as her captor sneered at her in growing anger. She showed no fear as she glared back at him. He gave her one last ominous warning glance and raced off down the corridor to help the others destroy their enemy.

Susan's voice travelled back to Mac and he brightened, filled with a fresh sense of hope. *She's still alive!* he thought as he turned and looked at the gun in his hand. "Let's just keep you handy," he said to the weapon as he tucked it into the back of his pants. He reached into the duffel bag once again and pulled out a handful of finely-crafted throwing stars, and then adjusted the sword before heading off in the direction of Susan's voice.

As soon as the Melonheads left the room, Susan tried in vain to free herself. She struggled at her bonds but they were tied too tightly. Her eyes had enough time to have adjusted to the dimly lit room, so she scanned the area, looking for something that might help her escape. She squinted as she saw something glint a few feet away—it was a bottle of MAYPEL syrup from Claudio's stash. She stretched her leg out as far as she could and kicked her foot toward it, but it was too far away. *Damn!* she thought. *A foot is as good as a mile.*

***

As Mac followed the smoke from the campfires as it travelled across the ceiling, he heard the sound of footsteps - a LOT of footsteps - headed in his direction. He knew after he had fired the gun that the sound would draw their attention, but he was too exhausted for another round with those beasts, especially the 'platoon' that was approaching, judging by the sound of the footfall.

Mac had a plan. He quickly stomped out the little campfires, darkening the corridor, and then wedge himself within a crevice in the wall that hid him from his attackers. From his spot, he saw a light, dim at first but growing brighter as it drew closer. A large comically-mutilated Melonhead (*It looks like Chuckles the Clown from television*, thought Mac) approached Mac's hiding spot, lighting the path with a torch. Mac tucked himself deeper into divot, not moving. The Chuckles Melonhead shambled by, followed one by one by the rest of the pack. They all passed by, oblivious of Mac's presence. He waited a few seconds after they had all passed and began to shimmy himself out of the crevice. *I need to lose some weight*, he thought considering the situation. Suddenly, as he reached for the hidden duffel bag, he heard a fresh set of footsteps. Without hesitation, he slid back into the hiding spot and held his breath just as the Gusher Melonhead came walking slowly, almost majestically, down the corridor. *Holy shit!* Mac thought as the hosed monstrosity paused directly in front of Mac. *He knows I'm here!* he thought and began to reach for the pistol and then paused. He held his breath for fear of being heard. The beast looked about, literally sniffing the air, sensing something. Sensing some*one*. He knew - he FELT - someone was close. Mac felt the Gusher Melonhead's eyes scan where he cowered, and watched as his gaze passed over him. The Gusher suddenly groaned, his breath hissing from his misshapen lips, and he continued down the corridor. Mac waited for a minute, although it seemed like hours, for the Gusher to get far enough away before he let go of his breath, gasping as his lungs filled with the stagnant air of the chamber.

***

Susan glared angrily at the bottle of MAYPEL syrup inches from her reach. Her basic biology knowledge that taught her that men have bigger frames and slightly longer reaches didn't do her ANY good. *Wishing I was a BOY right now is kinda stupid*, she mused as she tried to shimmy closer to the evasive bottle. *That damn Melonhead is good with ropes and knots!* She wondered where he could have learned basic skills over the course of the years. It was obvious where they got their clothing and their food, and Susan was thankful that she wasn't on this evening's menu. She pulled harder at her ropes when suddenly the tree root she was secured to shifted slightly, allowing her another three inches of stretch! She twisted around and extended her leg, catching the now-reachable bottle with the tip of her foot. She bent her foot around it and, with the dexterity of a contortionist, brought it close enough to grab it with her hands. She felt around the area for a rock and found one right under her butt. *I'm surprised I didn't feel THAT thing under my ass*, she thought as she clutched the rock and smashed it down onto the bottle.

She grabbed one of the larger shards of the sticky glass and began sawing at her ropes.

***

It was at 12:08 that Johnny had removed his shirt and wrapped it around the rock. It was now 12:09 plus fifty-or-so seconds, and Johnny wanted to wait until the last possible second before doing as his father had instructed. He cranked the valve of the propane tank and, after he heard the hiss of the escaping gas, pushed it down the hole. He looked at his watch another five times before it read 12:10. *It's time*, he thought as he sparked the Zippo, its flame performing a hypnotic dance as Johnny stared at it.

He grabbed the shirt-covered rock and held the flame to it until it caught well, and then he tossed it down the hole and jumped back behind a fallen tree, covering his ears as he waited for the explosion— which didn't come. Johnny didn't watch the flaming shirt as it fell down the hole, or he would have seen it get caught on a tree root and harmlessly burn out.

***

The torch-bearing Chuckles Melonhead waddled into the nursery. As he looked around for the intruder, he kicked something that was lying on the floor— Mac's duffel bag. He stared down at it as several other Melonheads followed him into the room. Two stayed and the rest moved on into the next corridor as Chuckles bent down a rummaged through the bag.

When he was satisfied that there was nothing useful for him, he tossed it to the other two that remained and continued on down the corridor that lead to the collection chamber, the flame of his torch casting an eerie glow as he walked.

***

As Mac followed the smoke from the tiny campfires as it drifted along the ceiling, he thought he heard the echo of tiny whispers, like children giggling, taunting him in what could have been a warped game of hide and seek. He continued his quick pace, but suddenly stopped and whirled around. He thought he had heard the whispering again, only a little louder or a little closer, and something like the sound of shuffling feet.

He stood for a moment, surveying the corridor where he had just come from but saw nothing. He didn't see the five young Melonheads that were stalking him emerge from the shadows, but his 'Coach Gordon' instincts told him otherwise. He raised the sword and spun around as he sensed their attack and swung as they lunged at him. His swing, which was slightly high, caught the first young Melonhead on the left temple, slicing off the top of his head.

Nice job on the sword, Blake, thought Mac as he contemplated giving him an 'A+'—IF he survived. *One down, four to go.*

The junior Melonhead attack team regrouped and were already on him before he could finish his thought. As they leaped at him, Mac lashed out, running one of them straight through the chest as a little 'girl' Melonhead slid between his legs and began gnawing at his thigh. He winced as she ripped the flesh from his leg and grabbed a spike from his belt and jammed it into her head and kicked her crumbling body into the wall.

The two that remained were slightly larger than the others. They circled Mac like a pair of rabid tag-team wrestlers looking for an opening to attack their opponent. As Mac swung the sword at them to keep them at bay, he reached into his pocket and pulled out a ninja throwing star and expertly sent it whizzing at one of his remaining stalkers. *Very good, Grasshopper*, he thought as the throwing star stuck into the 'kid's' forehead, disorienting him.

Seeing an opening, Mac wheeled around and took a swipe at the last teenage Melonhead—*Teenage Mutant Ninja Melonhead*, Mac thought and laughed—but missed.

This last nemesis was too quick, his animal instincts too well-honed. Mac dodged another lunge and pulled the pistol from the back of his pants. He barely had time to aim as the thing flew across the room. Mac fired, blasting the little monster in the head, dropping him mid-flight. Mac looked down at his watch—12:10—and realized he was out of time. He turned and looked at the Melonhead that was struggling to remove the throwing star from his head and shot him once in the head, removing the need to extract the star.

***

The sound of gunfire alerted the Gusher and the rest of the Melonheads. The noise was an unwelcome intrusion, almost painful in the silence of their catacombs. It was also an angry sound, one that spoke of hatred and torment.

At first, this 'human' noise of violence alarmed the Melonheads and they milled in confusion. Finally, however, the Gusher calmed the group. They looked at him expectantly, their eyes at once excited and frightened.

The Gusher took control of the situation. After nodding at the group he pushed his way through them, heading down the corridor that led to the source of the sound.

Confident now, the others followed.

***

Johnny gingerly climbed over the log he was hiding behind, confused. *Where was the explosion?* He crept back up to the tunnel entrance and carefully peeked over the edge. Nothing but a dark hole. He inched his way over a little more and hoped that the propane didn't decide to go off NOW, but he didn't notice that he was being stalked.

A teenage Melonhead was slowly creeping toward him.

***

Mac raced down the corridor. When he looked at his watch and saw that it read 12:10, he knew that he did not have much time. If Johnny had listened to him, the place should be incinerated in a few seconds. He ran full speed down the muddy hall and slid as he missed a turn and suddenly—WHAM! He crashed right into Susan!

"You scared the shit out of me!" he cried as she grabbed his face and started kissing him. He reluctantly pulled away. "Later! Later!" He looked at her and ran his hand along his face. "Your hands are all sticky!" and then he pointed to the ceiling. "We need to follow that smoke." He reached out and grabbed her hand and they took off down the corridor, trusting that the smoke they were following led them to safety.

***

The Chuckles Melonhead crept into the collection chamber, waving his torch in front of him. The room was dimly lit, but he could still see where everything was. Years of living underground and in the dark had honed all of the clan's senses. As his eyes circled the room looking for the escaped intruders, he heard a strange hissing noise. As the other two watched, the Chuckles Melonhead slowly walked across the room to investigate.

***

The Gusher Melonhead ran down the muddy corridor to the large hall where he had bound Susan only to find her bonds cut and her gone. He looked down to where she had been tied, only to find a handful of butterscotch candies scattered across the floor. Fluid poured from the hose that stuck out from his head as his anger grew. He lashed out at anything that was within reach as brain fluid sprayed across the walls. Through his rage and fury, he thought of the man who condemned them to this life and then his thoughts went to the woman who showed them compassion.

His destructive tantrum ebbed.

And he remembered.

CHAPTER TWENTY-NINE

Seeing the door lying discarded on the lab floor, the young Melonhead could only watch and worry. He sensed that his tormentor—the evil man—would be displeased with what Mama had done. And he was here, trapped, helpless, unable to help her even. The deformed boy looked around the lab at the other captive children. All their eyes reflected his fear. They all realized there was no help for any of them.

Upstairs in the Crowe Mansion, however, all was not well.

***

Marilyn spent the rest of the morning in a mixture of horror, anger and despair. After her first five minutes of torrential weeping, she got a grip of herself for a few moments. Had she overreacted? *Am I still overreacting? No, I don't think I am. What on Earth does Malcolm think he's doing—he stuck a pipe in the boy's head, for crying out loud!? A goddam pipe, he's draining brain fluid from him! And he's working for the government? The U.S. Government? How come I never heard of this before?*

Sitting on the edge of her bed, she did her best to come to terms with the horrors she'd just beheld...it wasn't just the boy with the pipe sticking into his brain and his innocent plaintive request for candy. No, it was all the kids down there, all of them. How in the world could Malcolm have gotten himself involved with a government project and never informed her about it.

She fell back into the bed and wept and wept. It was all too much. From time to time she got a hold of her emotions, but then, just when she thought she was past the worst of it, another flurry of images of the grossly distorted human caricatures down in their basement filled her mind and she broke down in tears again. Now she wished she'd never opened the basement door, wished she'd let Malcolm seal it shut and keep the key somewhere she'd never find, wished curiosity hadn't killed her cat, that she'd simply kept wondering about her husband's new batch of secrets, till finally, everything was over, concluded with and this nightmare went away of its own accord. Anything, literally anything in the world was better than the human torment she'd witnessed downstairs. The horror in those little eyes, the pleading on their faces.

The pleading of the eldest child—he connected to the dripping pipe. Remembering his voice filled her eyes with tears. Mama, he'd called her. And he'd pleaded for help.

For a fleeting moment, Marilyn smiled through her tears. *Mama. See? He's just an innocent child; they all are.*

Her smile evaporated. She was going to talk this over with Malcolm once he got back home.

And the removed door? What would she do about that? She smirked; to hell with the damn door. She'd taken it off and that was that, Malcolm could think what he liked—say what he liked—once he saw it. She was past caring. Besides, she wasn't going back into that basement if she could help it. Not till her husband was home and ready to do something to ease the children's suffering.

She left the bedroom, walked down to the living room, turned on the TV. Her favorite soap opera was on. This one time, however, the actress's and actor's glossy faces, their fashionable clothes and shiny cars and jet-set lives, their emotion-dripping voices didn't weave the familiar spell over her. After a while she got up, changed the channel. She knew the problem: she had enough emotion of her own to deal with. She channel-surfed till she found something that fit her mood: a news broadcast about the Vietnam War, pictures of burning people intercut with a stern-faced President Lyndon Johnson reiterating America's determination not to be 'cowed by communist cowards.'

"Freedom has no price!" Lyndon Baines Johnson stated firmly. "America's morality can't be bought and sold like soda in a supermarket!"

Sighing, Marilyn turned the knob down, silencing the president.

She sat on the arm of her chair, feeling a sense of desolation close in on her. And now she began feeling guilty. *How could I just run away and leave them down there like that? I really have to go back and do something.* But the thought made Marilyn quail: even if she did return to the bound children, what could she do? She didn't know; a feeling of impotence had swamped her. Reentering the cellar, however, seemed the right thing to do. But it was something she dreaded doing. *But I have to go, at least it'll make them feel better, knowing that someone cares about them. Oh, but if I see them again like that, I'll start crying again. Oh, oh, oh!*

She was saved from her crisis of indecision by the front doorbell ringing.

She sat up, looked around in confusion. The doorbell rang some more, a male voice called: "Hello... Mrs. Crowe? Are you home? It's Jory... Jory Crane. Your husband sent me to install a new door to your cellar. Mrs. Crowe . . ."

Marilyn remembered: *Oh my, what do I do now!?*

***

Jory Crane was a tall gangling kid in his early twenties. Mildly handsome, he had a large nose, thin lips and unkempt brown hair. A bit of a hick, Jory tended to look unkempt no matter the situation; even when wearing a tuxedo he looked untidy.

He was a nice kid though, Marilyn knew his ma, Sissy Crane, a plump widow who ran a cannery that that specialized in homemade jams.

Jory smiled at Marilyn. "Doctor Crowe said you'se expecting me, ma'am."

She nodded, then stared out past Jory (who stood slightly below her on the steps rising to the building's front porch) on the front steps at the man's open-backed blue truck. After seeing the new cellar door—a metal monster that made her think of a prison gate—Marilyn made out a female figure—a late teen girl—

in the vehicle's front passenger seat. She squinted. The girl's face looked familiar.

Jory caught Marilyn's gaze. "Oh, that's Alice Woods, ma'am." He looked back at the vehicle, "Hey, Allie, where's yer manners! Say hello, wilya?"

An embarrassed brunette head poked out of the car window. Alice waved. "Hello, Mrs. Crowe."

Marilyn waved back distractedly.

"We'se dating and she wanted to come along," Jory apologized. Then he asked, "Can I go have a look at the door your husband wants replaced? I gotta see if—"

"You can't do it today," Marilyn interrupted him with more chill in her voice than she'd intended.

His gaze turned confused. "But..."

"Come back tomorrow, Jory." Now her voice was cold. The chill wasn't because of Jory, who'd done nothing to offend her, but because she'd just remembered she'd knocked the door down into the cellar. And while it was true that the beds housing her husband's hydrocephalic 'patient's' couldn't be seen from the landing, Jory would definitely notice how much damage the door had done after sliding down the stairs and smashing into the cabinet. And yes (Marilyn was suddenly certain, a feeling of deep terror gripping her at the realization), he was certain also to wonder about why she'd levered off a door her husband had asked him to replace anyway (and which Malcolm was certain to have mentioned was still intact, and had likely given Jory the keys to open so as to more conveniently remove it.

And (this last seemed ludicrous to Marilyn, but it was a valid enquiry) how on earth was Malcolm expecting Jory to install a new door to the cellar without all the noise startling the kids? And once they started mewling and screaming (God knew the little dears were all terrified enough already) Jory here would dash down into the cellar to investigate and then…

And then, the hydrocephalic cat would be out of the bag.

Once she'd reached that realization, that preventing the installation of the new door was saving the children in more ways than one, the rest was easy. Normally easy enough to push around, Marilyn now found it the easiest thing in the world to maintain her stand on not letting Jory Crane enter the mansion.

(For a moment of contradictory emotional turmoil it did occur to her to let Jory in, to let him discover the children so they could be rescued. But then a thread of reason cautioned her. If she did so, she and Malcolm stood to lose everything; Malcolm would most definitely end up in jail, and she... *I'll be left with nothing but shame and ridicule.* But even beyond such selfish considerations, however, there was the possessive overriding emotion of her personal adoption of the suffering children as 'her own.' These hydrocephalic mutants, ugly and deformed as the all were, *belonged* to Marilyn. And they too clearly viewed her as their mother. 'Mama' the oldest child had called her. She masked a sigh; he clearly viewed her as more than just the 'candywoman.')

Hell, what was she to do? No, she wouldn't... no, couldn't let Jory through the front door.

"But, Mrs. Crowe..." Jory protested. "Your husband said I've gotta get this started on today." He scratched his head. "Doc sez it's something to do with keeping thieves away from his important research, and—"

"No," Marilyn insisted, hearing that infuriating, patronizing lie of her husband's further firming her resolve to deny him access. "Tomorrow. The house is a mess. I can't have you creating even more work for me."

"That's no problem. I always clean up after myself."

"No."

That final, defiant 'No' marked the end of the verbal conflict. Defeated, Jory, with help from Alice, left the metal gate in the garage. The pair climbed back into the blue truck.

Watching the vehicle roll off down the drive, Marilyn Crowe felt somehow stronger, as if this minor victory was leading up to a bigger, more important one.

Smiling grimly, she returned into the house. Now all she had to do was wait for Malcolm to return. They were having this out the moment he got in.

Simmering with indignation, she sat in the living room. Dr. King, the black human-rights preacher, was on the tube again. She stared at the negro's shining face for a moment, his expression intense, his mouth moving in an outraged silence that somehow still seemed louder than words, then got up to turn the TV off.

Seeing Martin Luther King depressed her; it reminded her even more of the discriminatory injustice being practiced right here under her own roof.

***

Malcolm Crowe arrived back home early. Staring out at his car pulling up into the drive, Marilyn knew Jory had called him: he was back an hour earlier than expected.

She shrugged, waited.

The front door opened and closed. Heavy footfalls followed. Malcolm's cologne announced his entry into the living room.

"What the hell is going on, Marilyn?" His voice was loud, confused and angry. The sour scent of stale smelt sweat danced under his perfume. "Jory called me. He said you asked him not to replace the door like I instructed. What was that all about? I thought we'd already agreed it had to be done as a necessary precaution against a break in?"

Watching him staring at her like she was guilty and himself the aggrieved party, Marilyn's anger overflowed. Her eyes blazing like furnaces, her facial muscles trembling, her breasts heaving with indignation, she leapt from her seat and boldly confronted him.

"I trusted you, Malcolm!" she screamed at him, her bottled emotions forcing themselves out in a furious rush. "I trusted you, and you lied to me!" She leapt at him, grabbed his coat, began blindly beating against his chest and weeping. "How could you do such a horrible thing? How could you?"

His face clouded over. "What are you talking about?"

She was angry. It was only rarely that she expressed anger, but this time her husband had gone too far, way too far and she'd had enough. "The tube in that little boy's head, how could . . . ?"

"How . . . did you—" Anger set over his features as he figured out what his sobbing wife had done. He peeled her off him and dashed out of the living room towards the cellar.

Marilyn dashed after him.

***

The young Melonhead with a hose sticking out from his head, craned his neck as he heard arguing from the top of the stairway. Dr. Crowe's voice, angry and berating, echoed throughout the lab as he shouting. The young Melonhead knew she was talking about them. He was instantly worried and scared, his body trembling in his fear. This was a new and dangerous situation, one he was unfamiliar with.

***

The couple stood at the top of the stairs. Dr. Crowe stared down in disbelief at the door crashed at the bottom of the steps, at the telltale screws and screwdriver on the floor (along with several dislodged chunks of plaster and wood splinters) then at his seething wife. Marilyn was panting, breathing out a mixture of air and indignation. He stared at her, at a complete loss for words. His expression was as angry as hers, muscles twitching like agitated worms under the white skin of his face.

The anger drained out of his eyes; he found his voice. "Marilyn, I've already told you not to mess with my research," he said, his voice soft and ingratiating, "there's lots of dangerous chemicals down there, things you don't know the use of.)

Marilyn recognized that her husband was about patronizing her again. He clearly felt humoring her was the best approach. Added to his layered lies, this angered her even more.

"What in God's name have you done, Malcolm!?" she exclaimed. "You told me you were trying to make them BETTER." Her voice grew louder yet. "You told me you were TREATING them!"

"They ARE being treated," Dr. Crowe lamely protested, more condescending than sincere.

Marilyn had had enough of his lies. "Stop it, Malcolm! Stop it! I don't want to hear any more lies. They're not experiments. They're CHILDREN!"

"Children whom no one will miss," came the too-quick rely.

"I will, Malcolm. I will."

Dr. Crowe's voice grew angrier. "Who are YOU to question the manner in which I perform my practice?" The boy's head dropped back onto the bed as the fighting continued. "The practice which has provided YOU with everything you have! This house—"

For Marilyn Crowe, that was the last straw: "What, you're blaming me for your atrocities? Blaming me for your monstrous 'research?'"

She lost her composure and hit her husband across the face, her hand leaping the distance between them like a striking cobra.

He jerked back at the blow, surprise leaping into his eyes. She'd never hit him before.

Still angry, Marilyn drew back her hand to slap him again. Anger in her eyes, her little hand flailed forward at his face again.

This time Malcolm Crowe reacted. He grabbed his wife's wrists and held tight.

"Let go of me, you bastard!" she yelled. "Let me go!" Tears were flowing freely down her cheeks now."

"Not until you calm down." His voice was cool now, almost mocking.

Marilyn didn't calm. She instead intensified her struggle to break free from him. She put all her strength into her efforts, pitting her might against his. "I can't believe you could be so cruel! And I saw the papers too—"

"What papers?"

She spat at him. "The government files! You're doing research for the government, aren't you?"

In his surprise at her accusation, she half-succeeded in wrenching herself free of him. She got her right hand free and slapped him again. Anger leapt into his eyes. He grabbed at her wrist; she leapt back, her hand swinging forward again.

"Let me go! I won't let you harm these innocent children anymore. I won't... No, I won't, Malcolm! They're my children! Mine!"

He ducked her hand, hitting his head on the door jamb.

Then, fighting to wrench her left hand free, Marilyn stepped on the screwdriver. It slid backward, pitching her forward.

Malcolm, dazed from banging his head on the door frame, saw her coming at him again, and mistakenly assuming it was another attack, got out of her way. He felt the sharp wrench of her wrist twisting out of his grasp as her body flew past his through the gaping doorway.

Too late, Malcolm saw the terror in Marilyn's eyes and realized what was actually going on, that she wasn't attacking him, but had somehow lost her balance. By then, however, she'd already slipped well away from his grasp and was tumbling head-over-heels down the stairs into the cellar.

Malcolm Crowe could only watch her go. Attended by his horrified stare, she fell in slow motion, like a water gymnast executing a roll in a swimming pool, her head cracking repeatedly on the steps with each turn of her body, her neck bending at an odd angle with each rotation.

***

The young Melonhead heard Marilyn shriek in fear.

Then, horrified, he watched her tumble to the bottom of the stairs. She rolled down like a ball and landed with a sickening thump. She lay motionless there, butterscotch candies spilled from a bowl previously dislodged by the crashed door strewn about all around her.

Eyes widening in confused disbelief, the deformed boy lifted his head and strained at his bonds. His eyes widened in shock and anger…

"Mama . . . mama . . . !"

All around the lab, the other bound children bore similar expressions of horror on their faces as they stared at Marilyn.

CHAPTER THIRTY

The Gusher's eyes widened in shock and anger as he looked down again where Susan had been tied, butterscotch candies strewn about. He threw his head back and howled mournfully, as the other Melonheads with him watched confused. As he slowly brought his head down, his eyes glared down the corridor where he knew they had gone. He took off after them, the other three Melonheads at his heels. The Gusher's pace quickened, almost to the point where the others could not keep up. His fury grew as he hastened along the corridor.

The Gusher Melonhead stormed through the dark muddy corridor with a superhuman fury as he followed the scent of Susan as he led the others toward the cathedral-like hall where he knew they would be heading. He practically galloped through the halls as the other three tried to keep up with him. He was NOT going to lose THIS one. He was not going to lose Susan.

As he ran, he remembered.

CHAPTER THIRTY-ONE

The young Melonhead threw his head back and howled mournfully, his young body straining at the bonds that held him to the table. He stared through bloodshot eyes at Marilyn's motionless— LIFELESS—body as it lay there. He trembled with a building rage, his chest rose and fell as breathed heavier and heavier.

***

The shock over what had happened left Malcolm Crowe in a rush, drained out of him like piss. Somehow getting a hold of his disbelief, he charged down the stairs. "Marilyn!" he cried. "My God! Marilyn!"

He reached her, knelt over her, grabbed her wrist and quickly checked for her pulse. Nothing. Her eyes were shut like she was asleep, her neck bent at that horrible odd angle, but she couldn't be...

Eyes growing frantic, he bent and listened to her chest. He heard no heartbeat. "Oh, God, my God, no, no, no, what have I done," he groaned. He was confused. He'd killed her? No, it was an accident; he'd been holding Marilyn's hand when she'd lunged at him. *No! She didn't lunge, she slipped... but will the police believe that? Who the hell cares what the goddam police believe? Marilyn isn't dead! She can't be dead! She can't be!*

Malcolm Crowe pounded on his wife's chest, fighting to resuscitate her. "Breathe, damn it! Breathe!" he cried.

No movement, no response. He put his lips to hers, and breathed deeply into her lips; he pressed on her chest, breathed into mouth again, pressed... She remained as lifeless as before.

He sat up, took her hand in his pressed it. His shoulders slumped in defeat.

"Oh, Marilyn I'm so, so sorry. I never meant to hurt you like this."

Malcolm's world contracted to just the two of them. He loved Marilyn; really loved her. Okay, so maybe, like lots of men, he was bad at showing his emotions. Okay, so sometimes she nagged him and he lost his temper with her, but that was normal enough with couples, wasn't it? You fought and then made up?

His sorrow shut the world about him even further, smothering him like a blanket. He was aware of sounds nearby, but they were unimportant noises. For a moment he remembered the children strapped to the tables and rage filled him. Yes, the little bastards were responsible for all this; they were the real cause of Marilyn's death. Yes, he'd make them pay for this, he'd... then his gaze slipped back onto Marilyn's lifeless face and the anger left him again. It was meaningless, everything was meaningless—this government project that was supposed to make him rich, had done no such thing. All it had done was take from him the one person he valued the most in the world.

Tears filled his eyes, sorrow his heart.

***

The other children in the room began screaming. Their cries were directed at Dr. Crowe, who had all but blocked out everything except the form of his wife lying at the bottom of the stairs.

The young Gusher grew silent, rage and fury building in his eyes. He pulled at his restraints, suddenly feeling in himself strength he'd not previously realized he possessed. While Dr. Crowe bent over his wife weeping, strong young muscles flexed against their bonds, slowly realizing their new power and becoming confident in what they could accomplish.

Finally, pushed to their limits, the straps restraining his wrists and waist tore and snapped and the young Gusher broke free. The deformed by took a moment to savor his freedom, sitting up on his bed staring about the room in wonder that he was no longer a prisoner, then his mind focused again, and he set to ripping off his ankle restraints.

Malcolm Crowe was oblivious to his prisoner's new freedom.

The Melonhead children screamed as the young Gusher tore the hose that came out of his swollen head from the IV bottle, letting it hang loose from his head so his brain fluids spurt onto the floor.

The young Gusher stared angrily at Malcolm Crowe's back. He felt strong now, and his mind was focused—as focused as the thoughts of the mentally challenged could be—on Dr. Crowe. Seeing the corpse beside the doctor filled the hydrocephalic boy with intense rage. He wanted to hurt Malcolm, hurt him badly, as badly as Malcolm had clearly hurt Mama.

Still Malcolm Crowe had no idea of the danger he was in. His horror was too great, as was his regret. It seemed impossible to him now, that something as 'little' as his decision to lock and bolt the cellar door had triggered his loss of Marilyn.

But how?

Malcolm was oblivious as the young Gusher pick up a large syringe filled with something that he'd watched the doctor administer to one of the other children that morning. He had no idea what the syringe contained, only that the girl jabbed with it had screamed and gibbered in agony for an hour afterwards. The boy grimaced; that was the kind of pain he wanted the doctor to feel. Holding the syringe like he'd seen the doctor do, he approach him stealthily, wary of the evil man despite his new-found strength and confidence. He was aware all the other children had fallen silent; they were watching him, willing him on, also wanting to see the doctor suffer.

The young Gusher reached the miserable crouching man.

He lifted the syringe high and jabbed the needle deep into Dr. Crowe's neck.

The blinding pain of being stabbed cut through Malcolm Crowe sorrow, he screamed at the penetration, then whirled round in shock. He was even more shocked to see the deformed boy free from his restraints, anger on his face as he depressed the plunger.

Dr. Crowe now realized the danger he was in. While pain made his head spin he wrestled the plunger away from the boy, then pulled the now-empty syringe from his neck. He stared at it in horror, feeling the effects of the drug cocktail start as it coursed through his body. Remembering what the syringe had contained horrified him: carcinogenic steroids, two protease-inhibitors, a mild toxin extracted from the tarantula, and there was that non-FDA-approved 'bulk-up' serum designed to double the size of cattle while also reducing bad-cholesterol fat in their bodies and increasing milk yield. Then there was also a heady dose of painkiller, which hadn't seemed to work on the little girl this morning (Dr. Crowe imagined the protease-inhibitors were inhibiting it too) and also…

The summary of everything, the long and short of the matter, was that Dr. Malcolm Crowe was suddenly in horrendous pain. His body felt like it was burning up everywhere.

He gaped up at the young Melonhead; the mutant child had a satisfied smirk on its stupid face. And its head… the pipe Malcolm had stuck into it a week ago, now dangled forward over his left shoulder, its open end ceaselessly dribbling cerebrospinal fluid down the boy's chest. And the kid's muscles! Malcolm Crowe was stupefied at how he'd not noticed this earlier (or had this just occurred—a rapid transformation brought on by the trauma of Marilyn's sudden death [yes, he knew they liked her…], but the boy's chest and arms were hypertrophied, the muscles standing out in stark definition, muscles that even for his young age put Malcolm's flabby body to shame.

The excruciating pain forced him down onto his hands and knees on the floor, till he was bent over Marilyn again, her dead face next to his. Damn, damn! Unable to look at her for guilt, he got back to his feet, and began staggering about the lab, while desperately clawing at his collar.

Around him, he was aware of a loud commotion, but was too wracked with pain to immediately care what was happening. His single thought was to find something to sooth the pain raging through his body.

***

Behind Dr. Crowe, after the brief celebratory pause sparked by their disbelief that their tormentor could hurt just like they had, the other children in the lab now went berserk.

They all began to scream in rage, a symphony of horror, pain and anger. The noise reverberated around the lab like the thunder of a thousand waterfalls, picking up additional volume as it bounced off whatever available surface would reflect it, then all of a sudden it peaked.

Almost simultaneously with the crescendo of pained angry echoes, all the children broke free from their restraints. This was no fluke; as a result of Dr.

Crowe's experiments they'd all long had the strength to free themselves, but had no idea that they could be free. Now that the young Gusher had showed them the way, they all stepped through the proverbial door he'd opened. Straps securing wrists shredded, their leather tearing like wet cardboard. Strong young bodies sat up, freed their legs. The children bared their teeth in rage, suddenly no longer scared of the middle-aged scientist. Now they saw him through new eyes: he was merely a pathetic pain-wracked figure staggering about the room with one arm pressed hard against his neck (where blood still dripped between his fingers), while picking up vial after vial only to stare bleary-eyed at the each one's label before discarding it to grab up the next.

Still, surprised at the freedom they were now experiencing, the children watched Dr. Crowe fumble about. Then, almost as one, as though guided by a nascent telepathy, the children reached a deadly decision.

***

Malcolm Crowe lurched about on shaky legs, grabbing at whatever surface presented itself to him in his efforts to remain upright. He was growing desperate now; his mind was fogging over like he'd soon fall asleep, his hearing faded in and out, and his body still felt like fire streamed through his veins. Uncertain where he was in his lab now, he had no idea where he'd find an antidote. He was unsure there even *was* an antidote.

Then the idea cut through his confusion: *I have to get upstairs and call for help. Someone from the emergency squad will know how to help me! I have to get to the stairs, but where the hell are they!?*

His eyes wouldn't focus that far ahead, so instead he squinted about blindly for Marilyn's corpse.

After a time of his eyes skimming over empty beds that seemed to have bodies moving between them(?), Malcolm Crowe finally spotted Marilyn's left foot.

He staggered towards it, only for his vision to be cut off almost immediately be the young Gusher.

They locked eyes.

"Not hurt Mama again!" the boy growled, the expression in his misshapen eyes baleful.

"I'm not going to hurt her," Malcolm groaned back, impossible pain wracking him now. *Oh My God, is this the sort of agony that little girl went through this morning? No wonder she was crying!*

He staggered around the young Gusher, who made no attempt to stop him, his gaze fixed on the bottom staircase step. There, for Malcolm, lay salvation of a kind, if he could only reach it unimpeded and somehow claw his way upstairs. Then he'd call the police. It didn't matter what they found now. Marilyn was dead; his world seemed to have died with her.

In his tunnel-like focus on the stairway beyond Marilyn's body, Dr. Crowe never saw them watching him, their rage focused on this evil man who had tormented them for so long.

He never noticed the hydrocephalic children rising en-masse from their beds..

He discovered the danger he was in too late. Suddenly aware of angry growls from little throats close by, Malcolm turned just as the young Melonheads swarmed over him.

Already on his last legs, he fell like a stone to the floor, was completely engulfed by the mob of enraged, slashing and biting children.

He began screaming as they ripped him to shreds.

Watching Dr. Malcolm Crowe die, a lopsided smile slowly formed on the gusher Melonhead's oblong head. Down the front of his body, the water kept pouring, splashing into a widening pool on the laboratory floor.

***

One by one, the young children stood up. Dr. Crowe, the TRUE beast, was dead.

When the children had stepped back enough so he could see his motionless, lifeless body, the young Gusher stood tall and pointed to the stairs. "Out!" he commanded.

The children, their dirty well-worn gowns covered in Crowe's blood, instantly followed his order and scrambled up the stairs. As the last one ran up and out, the young Gusher turned and gazed at Marilyn, a single tear running down his deformed face.

CHAPTER THIRTY-TWO

The Gusher Melonhead, followed by his 'crew' of three, ran toward the cathedral-like hall. He knew where the fugitives would be.

He was right: The Gusher burst into the cathedral-like room and saw Mac and Susan fleeing. He screamed and they both froze in their tracks.

"I am SO sick of this shit!" Mac muttered as he slowly turned to face his pursuers.

The Gusher was flanked by three other Melonheads; one with the physique of a gymnast, one wearing a grandmotherly housecoat, and one that looked like a deformed bear. Mac looked at each one of them as they challenged him and he pulled the pistol from his belt and fired three shots in rapid progression, hitting the Gusher's three 'stooges' square in the face.

They each hit the ground in a heap as the Gusher watched, blood and brain fluid pouring from their heads. The Gusher stood alone, staring, not moving, frothing at the mouth, barely controlling his frenzy. *Even HE knows he can't outrun a bullet*, thought Mac who seemed to relish the sudden turn of events. The Gusher Melonhead shuffled from one foot to the other and stared at Susan.

"Isn't payback a bitch?" he asked the Gusher with a smirk. The Gusher looked from him to Susan. After a slight pause, he spoke.

"Mama?"

Mac din't flinch, but Susan stepped forward. "Mac!" she cried. "Don't kill him!"

Mac looked at her befuddled. "What?" he asked, somewhat dumbfounded, "Because he said 'Mama'?" He shook his head and huffed. "No, I'm killing him."

"It's not his fault," she protested. "He was made this way. By Doctor Crowe. By..." she choked as she spoke, "my Grandfather."

***

In an adjoining chamber, the Chuckles Melonhead walked through the room, his torch lighting the way ahead of him as the other Melonhead guarded the entrance from where they just entered. He heard the peculiar hissing noise as grow louder as he approached the far end of the room, where some sort of sled—a toboggan—was leaning against the opening.

What Chuckles didn't know was that the room on the other side was filled with propane gas.

***

In the cathedral-like room where Mac and Susan stood in a stand-off with the Gusher. Mac still had the gun pointed right at Susan's kidnapper.

"Evil is evil," he said to Susan, "whether it was induced or he was born with it. It makes its own choice." He turned his head back to the Gusher, whose

hose began leaking brain fluid with more intensity. "Don't ya'? You won't stop killing, will you?" The Gusher snarled as Mac continued. "That's not a person, Susan. Maybe it WAS, but not now. That's an animal, tearing people apart." He glared at the Gusher. "Like some rabid animal! And you know what we do with rabid animals in Ohio?"

The Gusher looked at Susan. "Mama?" he said, more pathetic than before.

"And he's not making it easier for me by sayin' 'Mama' all the time," Mac said sarcastically.

"Mac…" Susan pleaded.

Mac was determined. "He killed Tony. Claudio. Dooley!" He paused and swallowed hard. "He killed my wife, Susan."

Susan looked at Mac in shock. "He killed your wife?!"

"AND your grandfather," he added.

"You're right," Susan said with a shrug. "Kill that son of a bitch." Mac smiled at her and turned his attention to the Gusher, who glared at them angrily.

"Bye bye, freak," Mac said with a smile and squeezed the trigger.

The gun barely clicked. It was out of ammunition.

Mac's face dropped as the Gusher grinned at him.

***

Chuckles approached the obstacle blocking the entrance, the hissing sound obviously coming from the other side of it. He thought to himself that he was going to be a 'hero' in the Melonhead world, whatever thoughts, or whatever WORLD, a Melonhead would have or be. He held out the torch and kicked the toboggan aside.

The sudden escaping gas hit the torch and ignited the air, creating a stream of fire directly to the propane tanks. They simultaneously explodedthe WHOOSH of the massive fireball instantly engulfing the doomed Melonheads at the entrance—as the fireball tore down the corridor and blasted up into the entrance tunnel.

***

Right above on the surface by the entrance tunnel, the young teen Melonhead that had been stalking Johnny pounced on him, tearing at his bare chest. Johnny had not lost his defensive football moves, and struck his attacker hard, sending him reeling back toward the edge of the hole in the ground. The attacker staggered as Johnny landed a side kick into the Melonhead's midsection that sent him flying over the entrance of the tunnel—just as the blast and ensuing conflagration shot flames from the hole like a cannon and hurled the teen Melonhead into the trees like a flaming rag doll.

***

The blast rocked the entire Melonhead lair, and the fireball that radiated from its origin tore through the narrow corridors, incinerating everything in its path. The nursery was the closest room to the blast. Flames bathed the entire room, roasting the helpless baby

Melonheads as they lay in their cribs, silencing their painful screams in an instant. The Melonheads that were in the feeding room fared no better as they were burnt to a crisp as they ate a final meal. Heat and flames found more propane tanks that had been secreted several rooms away, erupting them into additional flaming blasts.

The Gusher turned away from Mac and Susan as the ground shook, knocking things to the ground, even loosening some stalactites. He dodged one as it crashed to the ground next to him, and when he turned back, Mac and Susan were gone, fleeing down the nearest corridor.

They ran as fast as they could, knowing that they wouldn't be able to outrun the flaming wave of death as it quickly approached. Susan was breathless as she slowed down, but lifted her head and cocked an ear. Mac stopped a few feet ahead of her, turned and motioned for her to hurry.

"Wait," she said. "Listen. Can you hear that?"

Mac's eyes widened. "That's water!" He reached out and grabbed her hand. "C'mon!" and they ran off toward the sound of hope.

***

The Gusher watched, trance-like, as an orange glow came rolling down the corridor. He watched as the flames drew closer.

And remembered.

CHAPTER THIRTY-THREE

The young Gusher stood a long time staring at Marilyn's body. His lips formed an unspoken word, 'Mama', as he stared at the cigarette lighter that had fallen from her pocket. He slowly turned and gazed at the expanse of chemicals in bottles on shelves all around the lab. He snatched up the lighter and walked around the lab, knocking bottles from shelves and smashing them on the floor. He watched as the liquids pooled around the room. He sparked the lighter and lit one of Dr. Crowe's lab coats. As the flame caught the garment, he tossed it into the center of the room, igniting the chemical spill. The room quickly became engulfed in flames as the young Gusher darted up the stairs, braving one last glance at the one person who actually showed them all love. He ran out of the building as fire overwhelmed the cellar lab and spread up into the Crowe Mansion.

Young Gusher ran out onto the lawn and joined the rest of the Melonhead children as they stood and watched the mansion become consumed. Several minutes passed. A light rain began to fall as he turned to his 'family'. They all looked at him, waiting for direction. He looked at each one of them, their clothes covered in Crowe's blood. The looked like savages, but with an innocence borne of youth. Raindrops covered their faces. The young Gusher, their leader, pointed to the woods. "Home", he said as they all headed to the sanctuary of the trees.

CHAPTER THIRTY-FOUR

HIS home. The Gusher sprinted down the muddy corridor chased by the fireball. As the flames licked at his heels, he dove into a small crevice that had been cut into the wall. The wave of fire swept by scorching his body as he howled.

***

Mac and Susan turned a corner and found themselves running toward a fast moving wall of water. "What is that?!" Susan shouted as they ran.

"I think it's the back of a waterfall," replied a winded Mac. *Damn! I need to run more*, he thought.

"You think?!" she replied smugly as they sprinted. Mac quickly turned and looked back to see the orange glow behind them. They were almost at the waterfall.

"We have to jump," he shouted above the noise as they ran.

"Wait!" said Susan as they were narrowing the gap between them and the falls. "What if there's rocks below?!" The giant fireball tore around the tunnel behind them.

"We don't have a choice," replied Mac firmly and quickly as he grabbed her hand.

They closed their eyes and held their breath as they leaped through the wall of water…

… and burst through the front of the waterfall as they ripped through the water behind them. They plummeted down into the lake below as the fire nearly singed the top of their heads. They struggled to get their bearings underwater and swam to the surface, Susan popping up first as flaming bits of debris landed in the water and floated around her. Mac emerged from the depths a few seconds later and took a deep breath. "Mac!" she cried as she swam toward him.

He reached out for her as she came closer. "Are you okay?"

She smiled. "Yeah," she said quietly as they slowly swan to shore. Exhausted, they came out of the water and flopped down. They lied flat on their backs for a while before Mac leaned up on one elbow and gave her a smile. As she smiled back, she lunged toward him and rolled him onto his back, kissing him passionately. He willingly—and HAPPILY— reciprocated.

Suddenly, a pair of headlights interrupted their moment as Mac's pick-up truck pulled up and illuminated their interlude. The stared at the lights as Johnny stepped out of the vehicle with a proudly smug look plastered across his face after busting his father in a compromising position.

"All right, Dad!" he said, stifling a snicker.

"Hey, you found us," Mac said as he 'recovered' from his little make-out session.

"Yeah," said Johnny, pointing at the flame-spotted landscape. "You lit the falls up like a Christmas tree."

Mac stood and helped Susan to her feet. Johnny walked over and hugged his dad, and then walked back to the pick-up to the driver's side. Mac smiled as his son climbed in behind the wheel. For the first time, he was happy to be the passenger.

Mac helped Susan into the vehicle. "Thanks for waiting the extra five minutes," he said as he climbed in after her.

Johnny looked at him as he started the truck, confused. "I didn't wait five minutes." Just as Mac looked at Johnny with a MORE confused expression on his face. Johnny's cell phone rang. Johnny glanced at the screen and the caller I.D. read 'Ziggy', with a picture of Ziggy holding a chalice with the word "Pimp" etched into it. Mac smiled and shook his head as he noticed who was calling.

"You wanna hang out with Ziggy?" he asked.

"Nah! I'll tell him I'm still in lock-down."

Mac smiled at Johnny, and then cleared his throat. "You know," he began, "you don't have to stay with me all night."

Johnny smiled back. *I get it, Dad*, he thought as he put the truck into gear and backed it up.

As they drove off, no one noticed something large drop from the waterfall, and splash into the lake. No one noticed the shape of a giant head with a hose dangling from it.

CHAPTER THIRTY-FIVE

"Two! Four! Six! Eight! Who do we appreciate?" the busload of students and boosters chanted as the bus pulled to a stop in front of Coach Gordon's house. "The Bus driver! The Bus driver! YEAHHHH! THE BUS DRIVER!!" Everyone, especially Mac, was happy over the team's first victory of the season. Mac walked toward the front of the bus, high-fiving all the outstretched hands as he made his way to the door.

He hopped out and turned to wave at the kids as they shouted, "We're Number ONE!" and the bus pulled away.

This is the start of another GREAT year, he thought as he checked the mailbox before going inside. It had been a week since Kirtland was almost wiped from existence by the the Melonhead invasion, which, thankfully, had not graced and local or national newspaper.

The first thing he saw when he walked in, right in the middle of the living room, was Cujo eating Spaghetti-O's, his tiny head completely encased in the family-size can. "Hey!" he shouted in mock anger at the micro-dog. "Knock it off!" He smiled as Cujo popped his head out of the can, his furry face stained red with sauce and little round macaroni all over his nose. Mac laughed out loud and headed upstairs to shower.

About half hour later, Mac, still damp but fresh from the shower, came downstairs. He looked at the front door, which was open. I could have sworn I closed it when I came in, he thought as he walked over to it and looked out, hoping that Cujo hadn't escaped again. He had gotten out a few times before and either returned on his own or some neighbor brought him home.

"Cujo!" he called out. "Cujo! C'mon boy!"

When he got no response , he turned and went back inside, closing the door behind him. He checked to make sure the latch was working properly before heading into the kitchen to start dinner. As he entered the kitchen he scanned the room but didn't see the dog.

He could hide in an envelope, Mac thought with a smirk. He bent and looked under the kitchen table but didn't see Cujo.

As he stood up to inspect the rest of the kitchen, he DID see something he did not WANT to: the Gusher standing in front of him—in the middle of HIS kitchen—eating what looked like a small animal leg! The half-consumed appendage was jointed and dripped blood and mutant saliva.

Horror settled over Mac like a swarm of angry hornets. "Cujo…?" he whimpered. "Cujo…?"

Chewing on the hairy raw flesh, the Gusher's eyes regarded Mac with sullen anger. The monster was heavily burnt; large wounds ranged open over his flesh. He seemed too angry, however, his eyes gleaming with madness, to consider how injured he was.

(Here now, in Mac's house, the Gusher had only one thing on his mind —murder. He was here to kill the man who'd destroyed his home, destroyed his family, caused him such pain and suffering and sorrow. To the Gusher's malformed mind, the mutant's malformed head endlessly spilling cerebrospinal fluid on the kitchen floor, Mac was no different from Dr. Malcolm Crowe, the evil man who'd tormented him as a child. Yes! He was the same kind of monster! He even had a nice woman, Susan, of his own who gave them candy…)

The intruder flung down the half-eaten animal leg and charged. Mac had anticipated the attack, but still, he was caught off-guard. He saw the Gusher running at him, tried to get out of the way. His aging muscles, however, reacted too slow.

The Gusher body-slammed Mac, hitting him like a missile. He slammed into Mac with such incredible force that Mac went flying through the air and smashed into the kitchen wall behind him. Sheet rock broke. For a moment, Mark hung there off the floor, looking like a part of the wall, then he fell out of it, leaving a body-shaped hole in his wake.

He crashed to the tiled floor, his back and shoulders smarting in additional pain from his awkward landing. *Damn! he groaned. The mutant bastard! It feels like my ribs are cracked.*

The impact had rendered him woozy, the room momentarily swam in and out of focus. Knowing he was in danger, he staggered up, grabbing the kitchen countertop to stabilize his legs.

Back on his feet again, he sensed motion ahead of him. Shaking his head to clear it of fog, he looked up just in time.

Across the room, the Gusher was already in motion again, charging at Mac while cocking his left arm back. The mutant's misshapen face beamed with a kind of happiness like he knew Mac was easy pickings now.

Mac realized that if he didn't get his game together quick, he'd shortly be dead meat. And he knew what the Melonheads did to dead meat.

Fear of ending up like his dog Cujo energized Mac. Ignoring the pain of his fall, he swung into motion just as the Gusher reached him. The Gusher flung another southpaw haymaker at Mac's head. This time, Mac was ready. Anticipating the monster's punch, he shifted his weight just right and dodged the swing. Mac's head out of the way, the Gusher's huge bloody fist connected with the concrete facade of the wall instead, leaving another gaping hole.

Mac flung a punch of his own at the Gusher. He hit hard, packing all his anger and fear into the blow. The punch hit the Gusher in the belly, making him wince. Somehow, his hand was still stuck in the wall. Mac saw his chance: While the Gusher retrieved his hand, Mac hit him twice more to the jaw, each time with punches that would have made Floyd Mayweather Jr. proud.

The Gusher got his hand free and staggered back. The mutant was reeling, groaning in frustration and rage and from the pain of the contact. The blows had also scrambled its brains a bit.

Mac shook his head to properly clear it, then he glanced out into the living room. It was with intense relief that he sighted Cujo peeking out from under the couch. The dog was clearly unharmed, meaning the hydrocephalic mutant's gory lunch had come from some other hapless canine. Cujo looked pissed-off now, evil even, like he'd had enough of his turf being trespassed on. Mac smirked at the pet. *You lucky little bastard*, he thought, *you really don't know how lucky you are, do ya?*

Then happy consideration of his dog's survival took a back seat. The Gusher, pissed-off himself and way larger than life, was back in the picture. He took another hard swing at Mac, this time with his right hand (*Ambidextrous*, Mac thought, inanely thinking the Gusher would be a valuable player on his team), but missed again, leaving ANOTHER hole in the wall.

Mac couldn't help but be amused now. *This guy has the shittiest aim ever*, he thought. *I'll be fixing holes for a week if this keeps up.*

Oh yeah. And I'll be dead if I don't stop my thoughts wandering everywhere.

Mac's scattered thoughts were rudely interrupted. With his left hand, the Gusher grabbed Mac by the throat. He began squeezing, lifting Mac up off the floor as he did so like he was a kid. Mac kicked and flailed to get free, to no avail. Time to fight. He began throwing punches again: left, right, left, right, two upper cuts to the jaw, hard belly jabs, all into the rough bloodstained skin. The Gusher, murder in his eyes, refused to let go of Mac. Mac could clearly see he was hurting it, but yet it held on to him like a vise.

Mac began finding it hard to breathe. *Oh, hell no.* His punches grew weaker, but he still kept flinging them, aware that he had to get free from this terrible suffocating grip around his throat. White 'low-oxygen' alarms were already flashing in his brain.

(The Gusher grunted as Mac's fists slammed into him. They hurt, and hurt bad, particularly the ones to his jaw [each of which seemed to displace his brain], and when the man's knuckles dug into a burnt patch of his flesh. But didn't let go. He was pleased; he'd now discovered Mac's weakness —he would squeeze all the life out of the man, and it felt good, very good. His brain fluids splashing everywhere due to their conflict, he held, squeezed tighter still.)

Hanging there in midair, his strength fading, his air running low, Mac's eyes desperately flitted about the kitchen, seeking a weapon. It seemed useless; the knife rack was across the room, obscured by the Gusher's tall broad-shouldered bulk. There was another knife by the fridge but it was tiny one for paring apples. It might be useful, though, if only to break free, but how on earth was he gonna reach it before he blacked out? And he mustn't black out. That meant dying. And not seeing Susan again. And he had to see Susan again.

Then his gaze locked onto the top of the refrigerator: he'd just noticed his 'misplaced' home fire extinguisher hidden behind the Crock Pot. If he could just reach that, he could slam it hard into the

Gusher's head, force it to let go of him before he died of suffocation.

He stopped thinking in that direction: The Gusher had just cocked his right arm back again. Mac knew the mutant was about to deliver the final 'death blow.' Unable to help himself, Mac began preparing for the end. It hurt to go out like this, victim of some crazy creature that should have been put out of its misery ages ago, but . . .

He saw the victory in the Gusher's eyes. He shut his eyes, not wanting to witness his own end, then instantly jerked them open when his assailant suddenly growled in pain. Simultaneously, Mac felt the fingers about his neck loosen their grip.

He realized his demise had been interrupted. Fluid lashing everywhere from the hose in his head the Gusher was glaring down at Cujo who was savagely biting at his ankle. A look of murderous anger crossed the Gusher's distorted face. Forgetting his primary objective of killing Mac, he lifted his foot to crush the dog instead.

Seizing the opportunity of the distraction, Mac twisted in the Gusher's grip and grabbed the fire extinguisher from off the top of the fridge. Next, he cracked the Gusher hard in the face with it. Stunned, the monster released his grip on Mac's throat and stumbled back, its hose spraying liquid across both the fridge and oven.

While hacking in breaths like crazy, Mac saw with relief that Cujo was still alive and well, the dog now growling at them from under the kitchen table. Cujo leapt back in alarm whenever the Gusher's brain fluid splattered close to it.

The Gusher was still reeling, blood now dripping down his face from the dent in his head left by contact with the fire extinguisher. Quickly, while his huge adversary's eyes slowly focused again and filled with murderous intent, Mac considered his options.

There seemed only one that was certain to work. All the knives were still too far to reach, but…

The Gusher headed for Mac again.

This time Mac didn't wait for the monster to reach him. He too attacked the Gusher, lunging at his adversary. The Gusher flung a punch at him. He ducked beneath it. Once he momentarily had the Gusher blindsided, he quickly set his plan in motion: With one hand he grabbed the Gusher's head hose as it flailed about, while with the other, he inserted fire extinguisher nozzle into the Gusher's head hose and squeezed the handle.

Holding nozzle and hose tightly in contact with each other, Mac watched the fire extinguisher's contents flood up the hose and into the Gusher's head.

The Gusher went crazy as the foam entered his head. In torment from both the foam's chemical stinging and the abrupt increase in his intracranial pressure, he began swinging his arms wildly about, trying to grab Mac and free himself from the torment.

Mac, though, dodged every swing and swipe of the creature's hammy fists as if his life depended on it. *Damn!* he thought. *I should've been a boxer!*

The Gusher's head began to expand. He swung harder and more fiercely in his attempts to grab Mac and free himself, his actions propelled now by a desperate terror clearly apparent in his lopsided cretinous eyes.

Mac stayed one step ahead of each and every swing, bobbing and weaving about the Gusher (*Float like a butterfly, sting like a bee!* he manage to think), while holding on to the monster's head-hose for dear life. He also kept the fire extinguisher handle squeezed tightly down, kept pumping its foamy chemical contents into the Gusher's now increasingly inflating cranium.

The Gusher's head swelled like a balloon. Bigger, bigger . . . bigger still.

White foam began spewing from every orifice in the Gusher's head —his ears, his nose, even from the corners of his eyes.

Then suddenly, Mac heard a tiny squeak emit from the Gusher's head. Then a louder 'krak!'

The next moment, the Gusher's head exploded.

White and gray brain matter splashed around the kitchen (causing a mewling Cujo to dash further into safety beneath the kitchen table).

Then the Gusher's now-headless body, the 'ground zero' of the explosion, crumbled to the floor amidst a mess of extinguisher foam.

Mac walked to the body and stood over it. "You've been extinguished," he said in his best Arnold Schwarzenegger impression, and dropped the fire extinguisher onto the pulpy mess. Suddenly the body convulsed, sending a stream of blood into the air like a fountain of gore, covering Mac's chest and neck. Mac looked at himself and let out a sigh of resignation. "I just took a shower," he said, looking at a surprised Cujo.

As he bent over to pick up Cujo, Susan and Johnny, dressed in the Kirtland team colors and holding two boxes of pizza walked in through the front door. Their laughter quickly stopped as they looked around the gore-covered kitchen—AND Mac—and then to the headless body in the middle of the kitchen floor. Susan shook her head, and turned with a speechless expression to Mac.

"Susan…" Mac began, "… I HOPE you brought napkins!"

THE END

ABOUT THE AUTHORS

Bob Gray (screenwriter) – Charismatic and engaging funny man Bob Gray was raised in Mentor, Ohio by parents Robert and Helen Gray (deceased). The oldest of three, Bob was always entertaining classmates and performing in as many stage productions as possible. It was during his days at Mentor High School that he really began to get interested in television. While working in the school's television station Bob began to develop his skills as a director and as a performer in front of the camera. Shortly after graduation Bob took a flier and moved to Clearwater, Florida where he took a job as an audio operator for a little known station called "The Home Shopping Channel". Six months later sales were so big they began broadcasting nationally as "The Home Shopping Network". Bob was part of the networks first broadcast crew at 19 years old. In 1986 Bob got wind of a new shopping network opening soon outside of

Philadelphia. So he packed his bags and headed to the QVC Network. At 20 years old he was directing his second network. In 1989 at the age of only 23, he was offered a director's position at the Financial News Network in Los Angeles, CA. The opportunity to work in Hollywood was too much to resist. So he bolted to the coast. In between directing jobs Bob would dabble with acting, taking work in low budget films and in television shows. After 14 years of never getting his big break Bob decided to move back to Ohio and self-produce his feature film "Bigfoot". He figured that if Hollywood wasn't going to make him a star he would do it himself. And so far it's starting to work. "Bigfoot" has won film festivals all over the country and Bob garnered the "Best Supporting Actor" award at the Long Island International Film Expo. He resides in Los Angeles.

Solon Tsangaras (novelist) was born and raised in Queens, New York, where he first took up playing guitar, and then bass, being involved with many bands throughout the 70's and 80's. He majored in English and Communications, then went on to study Police Science, but went back to the music scene. He moved to Long Island, N.Y., in the late 80's, where he became involved with one of Long Island's top bands, Uncle Fester. Uncle Fester played the Long Island music scene for over twenty years, and has produced one CD, *Sofa Kingdom*. As an author, Solon has written the zombie novel *Detour to Armageddon,* and co-authored *Belly Timber* with Gary Lee Vincent and John Russo and *Attack of the Mellonheads* with Gary Lee Vincent; all of which are published by Burning Bulb Publishing. As an actor, Solon starred as *Oscar The Berserker* in the Horror Wasteland film *Belly Timber.*

Gary Lee Vincent (novelist) was born in Clarksburg, West Virginia and is an accomplished author, musician, actor, producer and entrepreneur. In 2010, his horror novel *Darkened Hills* was selected as 2010 Book of the Year winner by *Foreword Reviews Magazine* and became the pilot novel for *DARKENED - THE WEST VIRGINIA VAMPIRE SERIES*, that encompasses the novels *Darkened Hills, Darkened Hollows, Darkened Waters, Darkened Souls* and *Darkened Minds* (coming soon). He has also authored the bizarro thriller *Passageway,* a tribute to H.P. Lovecraft. His short story *Glory Holes* appears in *The Big Book of Bizarro,* his short story *The Tailsman* appears in *Westward Hoes* and was recently made into a comic book by Burning Bulb Publishing's comics division. His short story *Cocaine Connie* appears in the *Night of the Living Dead* tribute anthology *Rise of the Dead.* As an actor, Gary starred as George Pogue in the Horror Wasteland film *Belly Timber,* and has appeared in other films such as *Endor, The Goddess* and *Ayla.* As a musician, Gary has produced three CDs: *100 Percent, Passion, Pleasure & Pain,* and *Somewhere Down the Road.*

OTHER GREAT TITLES FROM

Burning Bulb

PUBLISHING

WWW.BURNINGBULBPUBLISHING.COM

BELLY TIMBER

From the writers of Darkened Hills, Detour to Armageddon and Night of the Living Dead comes a novel unlike any other...

In the 1800's, ordinary people learned the secret of the Kala and undertook extraordinary measures to rid the earth of this evil. This is their story.

For John McCormick, life on the Indiana frontier held nothing but promise. His settlement along the White River would soon become the crossroads of America. Friends and family from back in Ohio and other points east were all making plans to see what all the fuss was about in the newly-formed city of Indianapolis. Yes, things were good. John had his general store and his friend George Pogue had his blacksmith business. Claims were being staked and relations with the native Indians were amicable. The town was growing and nothing could be better... or so he thought.

In Ohio, an evil was brewing. The Lecky Family, a group of ruthless Mongolian nomads, had made their way to America and were practicing their cannibalistic religion of Kala with reckless abandon. No one was safe, not even John McCormick's family.

Burning Bulb
PUBLISHING

DETOUR TO ARMAGEDDON BY SOLON TSANGARAS

"An all-pervasive breakout of ghoulish pandemonium related
with unbridled glee and terror."
—John Russo, author of *Night of the Living Dead*

WHO WILL SURVIVE? WILL THEY WANT TO?

Enter a world where your best friend, your neighbor, your mother
or father, just aren't the same people you knew. But THEY aren't the
real enemy...

Join groups of survivors as they make their way across this
once-great nation that has been devastated by a man-made plague
created by corporate greed and fed by self-serving men who are
hungry for power and control.

Burning Bulb
PUBLISHING

EVERYTHING HERE IS A NIGHTMARE
Collected Works Vol 1.

"Pyles makes it look easy. His characters come instantly alive with the cocksure verve and swagger of rock stars."
- Daniel Knauf, creator of HBO's "Carnivale,"
Executive Producer/Writer, ABC's "The Blacklist."

The critically acclaimed author of Demons, Dolls and Milkshakes returns with fifteen tales of horror and suspense with Everything Here is a Nightmare.

From zombies in the old west, to a young boy tempted by the Devil. From vampires with romantic longing, to an abandoned lighthouse haunted by vengeful spirits. From a serial killer getting unholy justice, to a haunted English race car, Nelson W Pyles invites you to explore a landscape of fear, suspense and horror.

Take his hand and hold on tight. Remember that whatever you find here, whatever you see, no matter what you might think it could be... know this: Everything Here is a Nightmare.

Burning Bulb
PUBLISHING

GARY LEE VINCENT'S
DARKENED
THE WEST VIRGINIA VAMPIRE SERIES

DARKENED WATERS

When the world goes to hell, the chosen must arise!

As Talman Cane orchestrates a flood of epic proportions in this third installment of the *Darkened* series the towns of Melas and Tarklin are caught completely off guard by the deluge. Hell-bent on finishing what they started, the evil brothers return to the lunatic asylum to take care of the witnesses and add to the ever-growing army of the undead.

Aided by Lucifer himself and the insane vampire demon Legion, the stage is set to channel all of the forces of hell to come forth. In an all-out race to survive, Jonathan, William, and Amanda soon discover they are up against impossible odds as Lucifer opens the Gateway to Hell, ushering in the zombie apocalypse and the End Times.

Find out who will survive this cosmic battle of the ages in *Darkened Waters*!

DARKENED SOULS

Melas and the Madison House are about to be rebuilt.
True evil is about to be reborne!

Young ex-priest and vampire-killer William is drawn back to the West Virginian town that almost killed him, where his vampire arch-enemy Victor Rothenstein still stalks the earth.

The town of Melas lies destroyed after the battle of the End of Days. But why is wealthy Jackie Nixon so eager to rebuild it using the bone dust of murdered souls?

Terrible evil has visited before, but the Gateway to Hell is about to be reopened in a horrific climax. And this time – it's personal.

WWW.DARKENEDHILLS.COM

Burning Bulb
PUBLISHING

WOL-VRIEY
BIZARRO AND TRANSGRESSIVE FICTION

BOSTON POSH (BUD MALONE #1)

In 2028 AD, the USA is a nation ravaged by hungry dragons and dinosaurs. In Boston, Massachusetts, private eye Bud Malone is hired to rescue a kidnapped heiress. But nothing is as it seems.

Malone works to unravel a tangled web involving Boston Chinatown, a 200-year-old woman with a 9-year-old body, white robots, a human-liver-eating psychopath, a golem, a porcelain dragon, and a snake goddess with a crush on him. There's also a woman obsessed with chicken sex. Then Malone meets Posh Lane, a gorgeous call girl who's desperate to quit her pimp.

Romantic sparks ignite between Posh and Malone, but Posh's past suddenly catches up with her in a BIG way. To save Posh, Malone agrees to run a quest for Earth's new rulers, the Fork. But, Malone has no idea that agreeing to the Fork's odd request will send him on the weirdest trip he's ever been on in his life.

BOSTON CORPSE (BUD MALONE #2)

MAGIC CAN BE MURDER! - Drag queen Lucy Tang is back in Boston, and is hell-bent on settling her vindetta against casino owner Sookie Ling. And suddenly, Bud Malone, PI, has the case of his life to resolve.

When Boston's robot police force are baffled by a mind transfer case, they come to Malone for help. The one person who can likely help Malone out here is the witch Soledad Bathory. But Soledad seems know a lot more than she's telling him. It's a case not made easier when Malone meets Soledad's beautiful cousin, Josephine 'Slave' Bailey. Slave has her own plans for Malone, most of which involve teaching him BDSM and making him her new Master.

Oh, and Rick Rogers owes Sookie Ling a whole lot of money, a gambling debt that's going to be literally Hell to pay!

BOSTON CORPSE - Not your average detective novel!

Burning Bulb
PUBLISHING

WOL-VRIEY
BIZARRO AND TRANSGRESSIVE FICTION

VAGINA MUNDI

Rachel Risk is a professional thief with super-strong hair that can stretch like tentacles to manipulate objects. Ashley Status has both a digitally augmented brain, and 'muscle-purses' in her arms and legs in which she stores inflatable objects—cars, guns, rocket launchers, etc.

When Raye is framed as the fall girl in a jewel robbery, the pair flee Chicago's vengeful robot gangsters and take refuge in the Hotel Bizarre, where the gorgeous 'vagina singer,' Femina, is performing for a week.

But the Hotel Bizarre is even stranger than its name suggests, and very soon Raye and Ash are involved in an deadly adventure, a struggle for survival the likes of which they'd never imagined possible—with loads of deviant sex, drugs, music, and violence at every turn. And just what is the old woman in the skin desert really doing with all those cats glued to her walls?

VAGINA MUNDI—a Bizarro Hymn in praise of WOMAN!

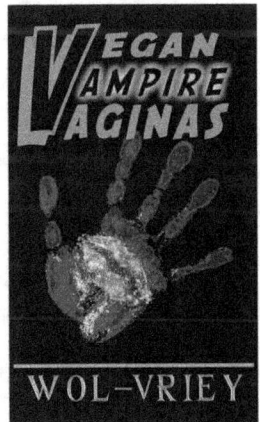

VEGAN VAMPIRE VAGINAS

The biggest bank heist in US history. And Tom Palmer can't remember pulling it off. And no, this isn't your standard case of amnesia. After a one-night-stand gone horribly wrong, Boston salesman Tom Palmer wakes up with a vagina implanted in his left hand. Then his day gets worse.

Tom is transported across space-time to a nightmare version of Boston, one where the Bizarro virus has transformed half the population into cannibals. Worst of all, Tom discovers that in this new Boston, he's the infamous gangster Pussypalm, wanted for robbing the Federal Reserve Bank of Boston a year ago. He also learns that the vagina in his hand is prophetic, i.e. it talks . . . after sex.

With 130 people left dead during his bank heist and six billion dollars missing, Tom knows he's living on borrowed time. It is in his best interests not to remember anything. Because once he does . . .

Burning Bulb
PUBLISHING

WOL-VRIEY
BIZARRO AND TRANSGRESSIVE FICTION

VEGAN ZOMBIE APOCALYPSE

In the post-apocalypse worlderness, zombies rule the earth. They're allergic to meat, and brains literally make them explode. Zombies now eat blood potatoes, parasitic tubers grown in the flesh of humancows corralled in maximum security farms. Two fugitives meet in the ancient ruins of Texas. The first is Soil 15-f, a womancow who's escaped her farm a week before she's due to be killed and her blood potato crop harvested. The second fugitive is Able Kane, former head necros food technician, now sentenced to death for heresy. But Soil is no ordinary humancow.

Unknown to herself, she's the vegan zombie agricultural revolution, and the zombies desperately want her back. And the necros equally desperately want Able Kane dead. He's fled with a forbidden discovery which will reshape the world for the worse if used. And Able is just hardheaded/misguided enough to use it.

MELANIE NEMESIS CATCHPOLE

In Springfield, Massachusetts, Melanie Catchpole is hired to fetch back a magic teddy bear worth millions of dollars from a warehouse across town. Problem is, the warehouse is down in Springfield's O-Zone-that totally weird sector of the city where Bizarro fell to Earth. The 'O' is a fairytale land, a place where dreams and nightmares literally live and breathe.

Worse still, the gingers—mutant cannibals—prowl the O. The gingers have already eaten everyone else Melanie's employers sent to get back the magic teddy bear.

Accompanied by the handsome but ruthless Doug Fisher (who she finds sexy but doesn't dare entrust her heart to), Melanie enters the O-Zone. Melanie and Doug are instantly caught up in an adventure they'd never have believed credible even if written as fiction . . . and Melanie's used to experiencing the very weird as the norm.

And now, additionally, there's a mystery to unravel: What does the dark, freezing-cold being called The Fixer want with Mary, the barkeep's daughter?

Burning Bulb
PUBLISHING

WOL-VRIEY
BIZARRO AND TRANSGRESSIVE FICTION

BIG TROUBLE IN LITTLE ASS

From Bizarro master storyteller Wol-vriey comes a truly weird western tale that will leave you awe-struck and on the edge of your seat...

In the town named Little Ass, tight-assed prostitute Rosa overhears a gunslinger's plans to assassinate rancher Edison Bennett. Once the badass Bennett learns of the plot, he ensures there'll be hell to pay for any attempt on his life!

Yes, it's going to take all of gunslinger Jude's shooting prowess, his eclectic collection of strange firearms, a trusty horse that requires an owners' manual, and the help of the lovely and invigorating Nell (who's EXTREMELY odd when the going gets weird), to survive the Bizarro hell that Edison Bennett unleashes in order to hold onto the land that he'd stolen from Madam Zizi.

BIZARRO 101 (A BASIC PRIMER)

Welcome to the strange place:

A collection of 37 flash fiction stories designed to introduce one to the Bizarro/New Weird Genre.

Weird, dreamy, nightmarish, absurd, sad, surreal, humorous . . . this collection of tales is all this and more.

***

"This primer is the very essence of any and all styles and types of Bizarro writing. Wol-vriey collects, distills, and bottles up these 37 tiny stories for your sensory enjoyment. This is an absolute must-read for anyone new to the genre, because it demonstrates the scope of what Bizarro is, and what it can be."
—Teresa Pollack, Bizarro commentator and blogger

Burning Bulb
PUBLISHING

ANTHOLOGIES
BIZARRO AND TRANSGRESSIVE FICTION

THE BIG BOOK OF BIZARRO

The Big Book of Bizarro brings together the peculiar prose of an international cast of the most grotesquely-gonzo, genre-grinding modern writers who ever put pen to paper (or mouse to pad), including:

NIGHT OF THE LIVING DEAD horror writers John Russo & George Kosana; HUSTLER MAGAZINE erotica contributors Eva Hore, Andrée Lachapelle, & J. Troy Seate and established Bizarro genre authors D. Harlan Wilson, William Pauley III, Wol-vriey, Laird Long, Richard Godwin and so many more!

From Alien abductions to Zombie sex, The Big Book of Bizarro contains OVER FIFTY STORIES of the most outrélandish transgressive fiction that you'll ever lay your capricious and curious hands upon!

WESTWARD HOES

Nine outlaw writers rode into town from obscurity to pen nine tantalizing tales of horror and fantasy, and leaving once they branded their own personal marks on the weird western genre and became living legends of the American Frontier experience.

Like drunken Indian scouts, the writers fervidly tracked down and captured the Western genre, tore off its fashionable veneer and ravished its exposed essence.

So belly up to the bar with your favorite soiled dove and enjoy perusing these thrilling tales of Old West debauchery, danger and desire; compiled by the publisher of The Big Book of Bizarro and featuring the bizarro novella *Big Trouble in Little Ass* by Wol-vriey.

Burning Bulb
PUBLISHING

ANTHOLOGIES
BIZARRO AND TRANSGRESSIVE FICTION

THE BIG BOOK OF BIZARRO SPECIAL KINDLE EDITIONS

OTHER AWESOME COLLECTIONS

 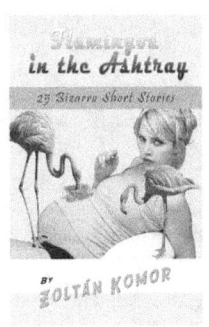 

Burning Bulb
PUBLISHING

DAVID J. FAIRHEAD

"David Fairhead writes compelling stories that offer very human characters and very inhuman monsters. There is no subtlety in Fairhead's imagination - he is simply dying to scare the hell out of you." - Nelson W Pyles author of DEMONS, DOLLS AND MILKSHAKES

THE FALL

Hopelessness... How do you protect your loved ones when Hell itself opens its insidious mouth?

Horror... Nightmarish Creatures invade your world and there is nowhere to hide.

Blood... How long can you hold out before they come for you?

Pain... Where do you run to avoid being eaten alive by monsters with a voracious appetite for your flesh?

Screams... While you selfishly run for your own life.

Questions... Who is to blame? Where did they come from? How many people survived...and how does the human race find the means to fight back?

THE FALL OF TOMORROW is man's last tale of desperation told by those that are striving to salvage some hope against a ravenous bastion of evil beasts bent on ruling our world.

DWELLING IN THE DARK

From David J. Fairhead, author of the FALL OF TOMORROW, comes DWELLING IN THE DARK- A soulful anthology of creeping terror to keep you up in the small hours with horror set in the past, present and future. Overlapping bits of puzzle fitting each other, before and after The Fall of Tomorrow.

A place where three children facing a monstrous foe can only pray that their bloody summer would just come to an end. Go back to the 1960's- THE COMMUNE where overindulging hippies use a mage's diary to control the end of the world, only to see first-hand that their drug induced visions have horrific ramifications. Where a young boy's visit to a haunted house becomes a lesson in RESIDUAL morality. The story, DEEPER- plunges two brothers into a sinkhole only to find they were being hunted by an insidious creature from its depths. Visit the old west as hero Dekker Collins battles evil gunslingers in DEMONEYE.

And so much more...!

WEST VIRGINIA-THEMED HUMORROROTICA

BY RICH BOTTLES JR.

HELLHOLE WEST VIRGINIA

From the heights of Mothman's perch high atop the Silver Bridge in Point Pleasant to the depths of Hellhole Cavern in Pendleton County, evil lurks within the shadows as the sun sets upon the haunted hills and hollows of West Virginia.

Bizarro author Rich Bottles Jr. blows the coffin lid off horror genre clichés with this tour de force cast of Eco-friendly vampires, beach-yearning zombies and sex-starved she-devils.

LUMBERJACKED

If you are easily offended or do not possess a truly depraved sense of humor, this story may not be the light summer reading fare you desire. As for the four feisty female freshmen stranded on top of West Virginia's third highest mountain, they have no choice but to experience the sick, twisted debauchery and perverted mayhem described deep inside the tight unbroken bindings of this horrific missive.

Lumberjacked takes the reader to a nightmarish world where character development and aesthetic integrity are prematurely cut short by the swinging axes of maniacal lumberjacks, who are hell bent on death and destruction in the remote forests of Appalachia. And at the climax, when paranoia crosses over to the paranormal, Lumberjacked makes Deliverance look like a family raft trip down the Lower Gauley.

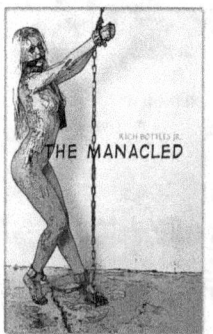

THE MANACLED

What happens when twin brothers lease out the former West Virginia State Penitentiary with the false purpose of filming a documentary on supernatural phenomena, but their true intention is to make a pornographic movie?

Chaos ensues as the disturbed spirits of murdered convicts, along with the reanimated dead from the neighboring Indian Burial Mound, take their vengeance on the unwary and undressed trespassers.

Zombies, ghosts, mobsters and porn collide in this bizarro tale from horror author Rich Bottles Jr.

Burning Bulb
PUBLISHING

NIGHT OF THE LIVING DEAD

Why does Night of the Living Dead hit with such chilling impact?

Is it because everyday people in a commonplace house are suddenly the victims of a monstrous invasion? Or is it because the ghouls who surround the house with grasping claws were once ordinary people, too?

Decide for yourself as you read, and the horror grips you.

All the cannibalism, suspense and frenzy of the smash-hit move are here in the novel.

www.TheJohnRusso.com

Burning Bulb
PUBLISHING

THE BOOBY HATCH

With NIGHT OF THE LIVING DEAD, John Russo helped blaze a path in the horror genre that has never been equalled. In this hillarious erotic novel, he blazes a path through the wild, zany Sex Revolution of the 1970s.

Sweet, innocent Cherry Jankowski works for Joyful Novelties, where she tests sex toys ranging from the ridiculous to the sublime. But she can't find love or peace of mind and her efforts are hampered by a Peeping Tom, an exhibitionist, a cross-dressing boyfriend, a quack psychiatrist, and even her own product-testing partner, Marcello Fettucini, who can't get it up anymore and is scared of losing his job!

www.TheJohnRusso.com

Burning Bulb
PUBLISHING

Bright little children, at school and at play,
until their minds are stolen away...

A Novel of Terror by

JOHN A. RUSSO

THE ACADEMY

THE ACADEMY

The Academy. It's every parent's dream, turning their little darlings into geniuses, superachievers, perfect little children.

And if there's a problem, the Academy fixes that too. It's a simple operation. Just a little device. Then a teeny pink scar on a tender little skull . . .

One boy knows the secret. Now he wants his mind back. But it's much, much too late. Too late for anything but the ugly feelings. The bad feelings. The messy sexy feelings. The knife-cold hatred, the murderous rage, for total, screaming, blood-drenching revenge . . .

www.TheJohnRusso.com

Burning Bulb
PUBLISHING

THE AWAKENING

For two hundred years, he has rested. Now he rises. Now he will be satisfied. Nothing can stop him. No one can resist him.

Benjamin Latham is young and handsome, his eighteenth-century mind wakened to a bizarre twentieth-century world. And there is the need deep within . . . an animal need, frightening, murderous, unholy . . . a vital need that must be fed.

And with his need comes a power over men and women to do his bidding, to quiet his dark craving . . .

Until the murders begin. And the inquiries. All suggesting the same hideous truth.

Now Benjamin must find a sanctuary: a lover, a partner, a friend. Someone who can share his darkness. Someone he can lead to . . . The Awakening.

www.TheJohnRusso.com

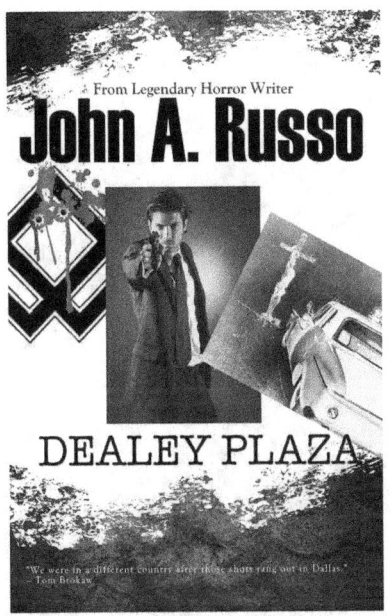

DEALEY PLAZA

From legendary horror and suspense writer JOHN RUSSO comes a harrowing tale where no one is safe!

Dealey Plaza is one of the most notorious places in America, and when youthful conspiracy buffs go there in 1964 to stage their own reenactment of the Kennedy Assassination, four of them are brutally murdered ~ the first victims of a hate-filled legacy that continues for four more decades.

The survivors of that long-ago Dallas trip, each of them now icons of the American way of life, are about to be honored ~ or killed.

Who will live and who will die? Will it be country-western star Lori McCoy? Her loving husband? Her scheming ex-husband? Or the case-hardened FBI agent and longtime friend who risks his life trying to protect them?

www.DealeyPlazaBook.com

Burning Bulb
PUBLISHING

"A sense of infectious fun, straight from the author's pen."
—Nightmare Library

From Legendary Horror Writer
JOHN A. RUSSO

LIVING THINGS

"Russo carries his talent for the horrific neatly over into the novel form."
—West Coast Review of Books

LIVING THINGS

Beneath the shimmering Miami sun sprawls one of the Mafia's biggest empires, a glittering world of lavish beachfront mansions, neon-painted nightclubs, beautiful women, expensive cars—and absolute control over the state's billion-dollar drug trade. But, one by one, its ganglords and henchmen are falling prey to a new rival. His powers are fueled by monstrous ancient rituals; his hellish undead legions slaughter mobsters and innocent citizens alike, his unholy lust for power is virtually unstoppable.

Now a burned-out ex-detective and a brilliant anthropologist must enter a gruesome, nightmare world to fight this master of malevolence and illusion. Their time is short, their weapons few, and they face an ultimate, terrifying choice - annihilation or the loss of their souls to the eternal torment of those who never die. . .

www.TheJohnRusso.com

Burning Bulb
PUBLISHING

ZAKARY MCGAHA
BIZARRO AND TRANSGRESSIVE FICTION

SEA OF MEDIUM-TO-HIGH PITCHED NOISES

The zombie apocalypse is changing; the world is coming to an odd demise; and a serial killer tries to change his ways and redeem himself before it all goes away. Now, Crabby has entered the world he left behind; the world of the undead. And things are changing. Everything will come to an end. In this new wave of the apocalypse, everything changes every five minutes. And death would be an absolute luxury. Psychological torment meets physical bloodletting in Sea of Medium-to-High Pitched Noises.

PARK MASTERS

Bad breakups, Bigfoot costumes, ghost bears, and more. Park Masters is a wacky, intelligent, quirky comedy about the power relationships have on people, good or bad. Also, it's just plain fun!

Burning Bulb
PUBLISHING

ELVIS PRESLEY, CIA ASSASSIN BY ANDY RAUSCH

"I can guarantee you. Read this book and you'll never look at Elvis the same way again!"
~ Douglas Brode, author of ELVIS CINEMA AND POPULAR CULTURE

SOON TO BE A MAJOR MOTION PICTURE

In 1970, singer Elvis Presley secretly met with President Richard Nixon. This new comedic novel imagines that Presley became a Central Intelligence Agency operative, eventually moving up through the ranks to become a skilled assassin.

Presented in an oral history fashion, the book tells us about Presley's secret transformation by the people who knew him best.

Did he fake his death in 1977? Was Presley involved with the Watergate scandal? The Iran hostage crisis? Communicating with aliens?

Read this book to find out the answers to these and many more questions.

Burning Bulb
PUBLISHING

MAD WORLD BY ANDY RAUSCH

"*Mad World* is dark, twisted, no-holds-barred fun."
—Jason Starr, author of *Bust*, *Slide*, and *The Max*

EVERYONE'S PLAYING AN ANGLE IN THE CITY OF ANGELS

Mad World tells the stories of a black hitman who doubles as a
university professor, a Catholic priest who longs to be a gangster,
a would-be author from Kansas, a gay phone sex operator who
claims he's straight, a group of rich twentysomethings playing a
deadly game of life and death, a vicious Mafia boss, and a sleazy
Hollywood movie director. As each of their stories intersect, the
body count piles up and the action comes nonstop in this tense,
white-knuckle thriller by first-time author Andy Rausch.

"A wild ride. If you like it gangster, *Mad World* delivers."
—Daniel Birch, author of *Get Some*

Burning Bulb
PUBLISHING

BLOODLETTING: A TALE OF REVENGE BY ANDY RAUSCH

"Relentless... Addictive... The kind of nightmare you don't want
to wake up from."
—Heywood Gould, screenwriter of *Rolling Thunder*

He was just an average Joe. But when he finds his family held at
gunpoint by merciless thugs, he's told he must murder a Mafia
chieftain if he ever wishes to see his loved ones again.

Against all odds, Joe keeps his end of the bargain, but the criminals
don't. Now at his wits end, Joe is pushed beyond his breaking point
and forced to exact bloody revenge against those who've done him
and his family wrong in this powerful and violent novella by author
Andy Rausch (*Mad World*).

"Andy Rausch has a tight noir style that combines gritty, realistic drama
with a cinematic flair that makes for a powerful, compelling (somewhat
Stephen Kingesque), authentically visual reading experience."
—Stephen Spignesi, author of *Dialogues*

Burning Bulb
PUBLISHING

THE TAILSMAN

From the creators of *The Big Book of Bizarro* and *Westward Hoes* comes a new comic unlike anything you have ever seen!

He's hot on the trail, looking for some *tail*...

Sly Franko was a man of the West, a forger of the wild frontier. Like the Country Western song that would be written years after he died, the words, "Faster horses, younger women, and more money," seemed to be the anthem of this horn dog cowboy.

Franko would ride into town on a blazing saddle, find the closest saloon to wet the whistle, belly up to a good card game, and find him a hot-loving hussy to get his cowpoke on with.

However, Sly might have met his match when a visit to bathroom leads to terror and death. Can Sly and his poker buddies solve the mystery before more of the townsfolk are murdered? Find out in this exciting premier issue of *The Tailsman*!

WWW.BURNINGBULBCOMICS.COM

THE HAGS OF BLACK COUNTY

by Michelle Bowser

Ruled by a committee of Hags, and fueled by toothless rivalries, Black County lurks just far enough out of the way to be completely unnoticed by the rest of civilization. Its inhabitants have been mentally warped for generations and the land itself seems to have the power to drive anyone unlucky enough to visit into ridiculous hillbilly madness. When a construction Company needs to bury a pipeline through its ludicrous hills and valleys, a twisted charm goes to work and every aspect of already bizarre Black County life takes a gory turn for the hysterical. Take a preposterous trip along with its citizens, both native and new, through escapades such as the Hag parade, the grand opening of Madame Skunk's House of Ill Repute, the demolition derby riot and the rabid, zombie clown apocalypse.

THE ABANDONED SOUL

by Daniel Sellers

After spending most of his 20s in a drug and alcohol fueled daze, a young man finally hits rock bottom. Having used up his friends and their good graces, he ends up squatting in an abandoned house. Forcibly sobering he begins to realize that he is not alone in this abandoned house. Left with one last friend and a mountain of regrets, he must decide if this presence is a guilty conscience, or a malicious hunter.

WE WISH YOU A HAPPY KILLDAY

by Jason Heroux

"We Wish You a Happy Killday" is the story of an international b eloved holiday called "Killday" where one day a year everyone over the age of fifteen is permitted to register for a license allowing them to kill one other person. But this year Chad Ovenstock doesn't feel like killing anyone. His friends and family urge him to participate in the festivities, but he can't seem to get into the holiday spirit. On the day before Killday Chad comes in contact with Ambrose, an old friend who suffered a nervous breakdown and is now part of The One Ant Army, a mysterious cult dedicated to making the future disappear. When the holiday finally arrives Chad refuses to participate and tries to survive on his own, surrounded by constant gunfire, countless corpses, and the nagging suspicion that Ambrose may have secretly brainwashed him into becoming a member of The One Ant Army cult.

Burning Bulb